In the Charm

Editor: Talia Leduc

ISBN-13: 9781990590108

Give feedback on the book at:
lorhainneeckhart.le@gmail.com

Twitter: @LEckhart
Facebook: AuthorLorhainneEckhart

Printed in the U.S.A

IN THE CHARM

The Friessens

LORHAINNE ECKHART

When Chris finds himself on the wrong side of the law in a small South Dakota town, the local cops tell him to hit the road. But that's easier said than done when he meets JD, the sheriff's irresistible daughter...

When stubbornly independent Chris Friessen decides to pack up and travel the country on the back of his Harley, he doesn't expect that his decision to see the "real USA" will cost him in ways he can't imagine. He soon finds himself face down on some backroad, cuffed by small-town cops. To make matters worse, he's told to keep moving, but when he meets the incredibly sexy daughter of the sheriff, Chris can't resist doing exactly the opposite—even after realizing that the sheriff's deputy is head over heels in love with her.

JD is the daughter of a South Dakota small-town sheriff, teased by locals that if she were ever to consider marrying, she'd have a line of suitors around the block. But she's not interested, as the only man she's ever loved up and left, and her father was behind it. When she drives up on her father and his deputy toying with the extremely attractive redheaded Chris Friessen, she can't resist tossing him an invitation to dinner, and she never expects that he'll take her up on it.

Now, Chris may find that the irresistible JD comes with a lot more than he's bargained for.

Click here to download the complete Friessen Legacy Series checklist and series reading order

The Outsider Series

The Forgotten Child (Brad and Emily)
A Baby and a Wedding
Fallen Hero (Andy, Jed, and Diana)
The Search
The Awakening (Andy and Laura)
Secrets (Jed and Diana)

Runaway (Andy and Laura)
Overdue
The Unexpected Storm (Neil and Candy)
The Wedding (Neil and Candy)

The Friessens: A New Beginning

The Deadline (Andy and Laura)
The Price to Love (Neil and Candy)
A Different Kind of Love (Brad and Emily)
A Vow of Love, A Friessen Family Christmas

The Friessens

The Reunion
The Bloodline (Andy & Laura)
The Promise (Diana & Jed)
The Business Plan (Neil & Candy)
The Decision (Brad & Emily)
First Love (Katy)
Family First
Leave the Light On
In the Moment
In the Family: A Friessen Family Christmas
In the Silence
In the Stars
In the Charm
Unexpected Consequences
It Was Always You
The First Time I Saw You
Welcome to My Arms
Welcome to Boston
I'll Always Love You
Ground Rules

A Reason to Breathe
You Are My Everything
Anything For You
The Homecoming includes FREE short story When They
Were Young
Stay Away From My Daughter
The Bad Boy
A Place to Call Our Own
The Visitor
All About Devon
Long Past Dawn
How to Heal a Heart
Keep Me In Your Heart

Want to know how all the series are linked? Stop by my blog for all the details: http://www.lorhainneeckhart.com/what-is-the-reading-order-of-your-books/

Now Available at a specially reduced price, The Friessen Legacy Collections:

1) The Outsider Series: The Complete Omnibus Collection
2) The Friessens A New Beginning: The Collection
3) The Friessens Books 1 - 5 Box Set
4) The Friessens Books 6 -8
5) The Friessen Books 9 - 11
6) The Friessen Books 12 - 14
7) The Friessen Books 15 - 18
8) The Friessen Books 19 -21
9. The Friessen Books 22 - 24
10) The Friessens Books 25 - 27
11) The Friessens Books 28 - 31

The Friessen Family

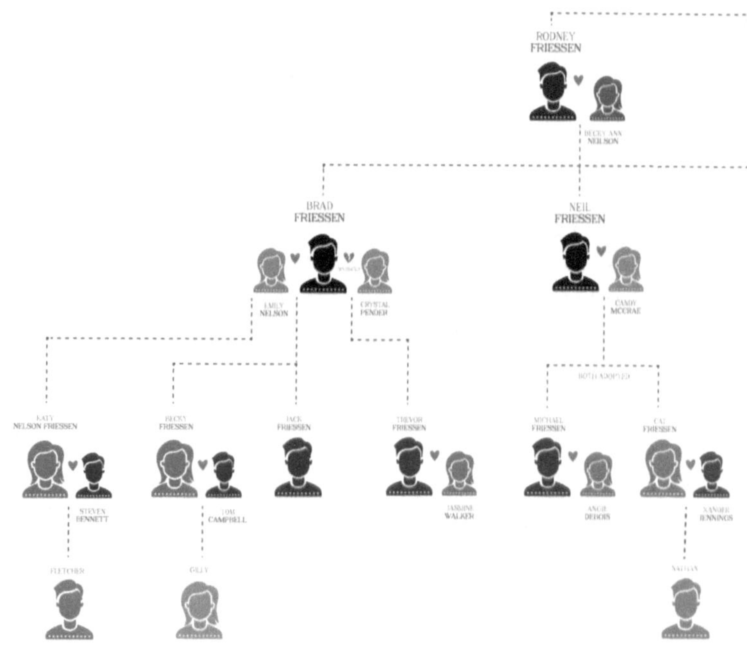

The Outsider Series

THE FORGOTTEN CHILD	BRAD & EMILY
A BABY AND A WEDDING	BRAD & EMILY & and her two brothers & Becky
FALLEN HERO	JED, DIANA & ANDY
THE SEARCH	JED, DIANA & ANDY
THE AWAKENING	ANDY & LAURA

The Outsider Series

SECRETS	DIANA & JED with the entire Friessen Family
RUNAWAY	ANDY & LAURA
OVERDUE	JED & DIANA
THE UNEXPECTED STORM	NEIL & CANDY
THE WEDDING	NEIL & CANDY and the entire Friessen Family

The Friessens: A New Beginning

THE DEADLINE	ANDY & LAURA
THE PRICE TO LOVE	NEIL & CANDY
A DIFFERENT KIND OF LOVE	BRAD & EMILY
A VOW OF LOVE	THE ENTIRE
A FRIESSEN FAMILY CHRISTMAS	FRIESSEN FAMILY

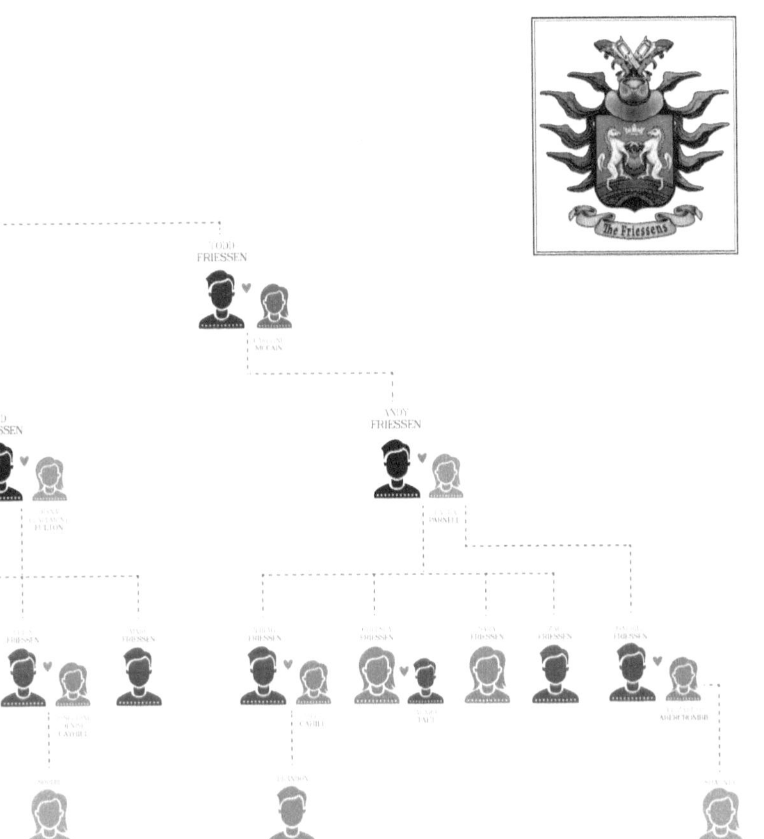

The Friessens

THE ENTIRE FRIESSEN FAMILY	
ANDY & LAURA	
JED & DIANA	
NEIL & CANDY	
BRAD & EMILY	
KATY & STEVEN	
KATY & STEVEN	

The Friessens

LEAVE THE LIGHT ON	KATY & STEVEN
IN THE MOMENT	BECKY & TOM
IN THE FAMILY	THE ENTIRE FRIESSEN FAMILY
IN THE SILENCE	CAL & XANDER
IN THE STARS	DANNY & EVIE
IN THE CHARM	CHRIS & ED
UNEXPECTED CONSEQUENCES	CHRIS & ED

The Friessens

IT WAS ALWAYS YOU	KATY & STEVEN
THE FIRST TIME I SAW YOU	GABRIEL & ELIZABETH
WELCOME TO MY ARMS	CHELSEA & ALARIC
WELCOME TO BOSTON	PAIGE & MORGAN
I'LL ALWAYS LOVE YOU	JEREMY
GROUND RULES	JEREMY & TIFFY
A REASON TO BREATHE	TREVOR & JASMINE
YOU ARE MY EVERYTHING	MICHAEL & ANGIE
ANYTHING FOR YOU	
THE HOMECOMING	THE ENTIRE FRIESSEN FAMILY

Chapter One

Of all the decisions twenty-three-year-old Chris Friessen had made, his latest was likely to cost him in ways he hadn't even begun to imagine, considering the flashing sheriff's lights in his side mirrors. The car had ridden up on his ass, its siren blasting until he pulled over, and he was now parked on a road—scratch that, a secondary highway in the middle of nowhere.

Actually, it wasn't really nowhere. He'd covered roughly two hundred and twenty miles that day, with the heat and sun beating down, but he couldn't rightly pinpoint exactly which county or, for that matter, state he was in. He'd pulled off the main highway crossing the country from east to west, and now he was having a hard time remembering whether he was in one of the Dakotas or in Montana, which, in his mind, put him in the middle of nowhere.

"Turn off the bike and step off! Show me your hands." The deep voice of what sounded like one pissed-off cop boomed over the loudspeaker, but the twang did little to help Chris figure out exactly where he was.

He turned off his bike and kicked the support stand, then lifted his leg over slowly and stepped down, his hands going right to the strap of his helmet to lift it off.

"I said show me your hands, asshole!" the cop yelled, shooting a bolt of fear straight through Chris.

His hands, suddenly with a mind of their own, jabbed in the air high enough that there could be no mistake he was following instructions to a T. His heart was hammering, feeling the heat of the approaching cop. He could just make out his feet scraping the pavement, and he was straining to hear everything through his thick helmet—the radio, the tick of something, and the wind that did little to cool off this scorcher of a day. He wanted to explain to this cop that he was…what, a great guy just seeing the country, traveling from state to state? Why exactly had he been pulled over?

"If you'll just let me take off my helmet—" He didn't get to finish, because rough hands gripped his left wrist, and metal cuffs were slapped on as his other arm was twisted back roughly. The pinch of the metal shot through his arm. "Ah, fuck, what the hell?" he yelled from the sudden bite. Then his helmet was pulled off and dumped on the asphalt. The smash was instant, and he saw the visor crack. The sound was one he'd never forget. He had dished out two hundred and fifty dollars for that thing— and it had been on sale.

"You watch your mouth," the cop snapped, his hand on him.

Chris landed roughly on the ground, face down, the heat from the midday sun on the blacktop burning into him through the black leather jacket he always wore on his bike. He struggled to keep his face off the scorching road as he turned his head, taking in his Harley, a Forty-Eight Special with a long wheel base that screamed badass class.

Chris had fallen in love with the bike the moment he'd seen it through the window of the Arlington bike shop.

A second cop was unfastening the gear tied on the back of the bike and going through the compartment where his bag, wallet, ID, insurance, and everything of value were stashed.

"You mind telling me why you pulled me over?" Chris said, turning his head, still waiting for the cops to answer his other questions. Of course, they knew what they were doing.

The cop who'd cuffed him and put him on the ground was in a black uniform shirt with a badge pinned to his chest. He was wearing dark shades and was a lot rounder in the middle, and he worked a piece of gum as he holstered his weapon and then leaned down to Chris. "You packing? Got any weapons on you?"

Rough hands patted him down, grabbing him in places no stranger had any business putting his hands.

"No," Chris said. "Now how about answering my question? Why did you pull me over?" He was sure he hadn't been speeding. He'd made a point of keeping an eye out for any signs of the speed limit, enjoying every moment of the secondary back country. He'd planned for this, the only way to see the small towns and counties no one ever stopped in. But there was a moment now, as he understood his current predicament, that he realized maybe taking this route hadn't been one of his smarter choices.

The older cop said nothing as the other one handed him Chris's license with a scowl.

Chris had to strain his neck, holding his head up, feeling the burn of the pavement on his chin. "Seriously, guys, I know what my rights are. Why exactly am I cuffed and on the ground in the middle of nowhere? My mother's a lawyer. You think I'm not well aware of the bullshit going on here?"

He stopped talking, running everything through his head—the what, the where, and the how. He was thankful he'd actually listened to his mom when she gave him the talk about his rights, though it had been his brother Danny, who was just finishing up law school, who had really driven home how often people's rights were violated, especially the rights of those who didn't have a clue what their rights were. That had been an interesting talk over one too many beers. Now here he was, in that exact worst-case scenario, and he suddenly felt like it could end badly for him.

The cops said nothing, but he could hear them behind him as he racked his brain, trying to figure out what he'd done. They had to have a reason to pull him over and cuff him. Then there was the really big problem: They hadn't even read him his rights. He wanted to remind them, but all that came out was a groan as he felt the pinch of his cuffed wrists and the pull in his shoulders, a rock biting into his hip. It was enough of a wakeup call that he knew reasoning with those two assholes wouldn't work, not in this situation.

"Christopher Friessen, from North Lakewood in Washington State," the cop drawled. He held up Chris's registration and insurance, or so it seemed, from the papers he was holding. It was beginning to seem more and more that this was a fishing expedition—but for what, he didn't have a clue. Probably something he wasn't going to like.

"The name's Chris," he snapped. No one called him Christopher but his mother—and his dad, grandparents, aunts, uncles, and brothers, Danny and Mark, but only when they wanted to push all his buttons. His brothers knew the effort he was making to get everyone to cut it out and stop calling him something he didn't see himself as. It was a baby name, a little kid's name, which didn't fit badass Chris, who rode a Harley and had saved up to travel the country and really see it instead of reading about it.

"You're a long way from home, there, Christopher. Mind telling me what you're doing out this way?"

Seriously, what the fuck? He had to bite the words back, hating this feeling of being toyed with. "The name's Chris, I already told you, and I'm just passing through. Didn't think that was a crime. Now how about uncuffing me and telling me why the fuck you're treating me like some criminal?"

He realized as soon as the words were out of his mouth that it had likely been the wrong thing to say. He turned his head right and then left, seeing both their badges pinned to their chests. The cop by his bike wasn't as old as the one who had pinned him down on the ground and cuffed him. He was dark haired, tall, and the way he stared down, unsmiling, his face seemed made of granite. Chris realized this was a lawman whose gun he'd never want to find himself on the wrong side of, considering his dark, completely unimpressed expression.

"How about you settle on down there, boy, and mind your manners?" said the other cop as his booted foot kicked Chris in the shin. He was older, with a deeper voice and a potbelly.

Chris grunted from the stab of pain. "Fuck!" he muttered under his breath and pulled at his wrists, turning his head to the side again, seeing the cowboy boot that would likely kick him again. He dragged his gaze up, taking in the older cop, who wore a ball cap over what Chris thought was a bald head. He was maybe his dad's age.

Just then, he heard a car and spotted a rusty older-model import slowing as it came closer. The older cop stepped into the road and lifted his hand, and Chris couldn't see much as the car stopped just behind him.

The cop leaned in the window. "Hey there, baby girl. What're you doing out this way?"

The way the cop's voice changed from asshole to sappy had Chris wanting to roll his eyes. For a second, he considered calling out to the driver to…what, help him out of his predicament?

"Just finished delivering meals to some of the shut-ins and was heading home. Could ask you the same, Daddy. What're you doing all the way out here, and what did that man do?" Her voice was soft and sassy, and Chris wished he could see her face over the rusty fender and the bald tires, which were the only things in his view.

"Oh, that's nothing for you to worry your pretty little head about. Just a routine traffic stop."

Routine, his ass! There was nothing routine about this stop or the fact that he was cuffed, lying face down on the burning pavement in what he was sure was ninety-degree heat on this late afternoon in early August.

"If this is just routine, then how about uncuffing me and letting me up?" he snapped.

Rough hands suddenly gripped his arm and pulled him up, and he had to stifle a groan at his wrenched shoulder. He took in the babe in the car. She had long dirty-blond hair and a killer smile—a knockout, from what he could see with the windshield between them. He heard the key and felt the hand on his wrist again as the cuff loosened, and he was suddenly free.

On instinct, he reached for his wrist and rubbed, rolling his shoulders as he turned around. He couldn't imagine spending hours with his arms cuffed behind him. Having felt the bite and how tight they were, he realized he really had been at the mercy of the cop restraining him.

He couldn't see the eyes of the younger cop who'd uncuffed him from behind his shades. The man stepped away from Chris and over to the car, lifting his hand and smiling at the killer babe.

"Hey there, JD," he said. "I'm sure the good folks of Martin appreciate all the help you're giving." The way his voice had changed to overly affectionate was ridiculous.

"Ah, thanks, Ray. Just doing my part, is all. We have a lot of seniors who just can't get out anymore." She had a brilliant smile, and the cop actually touched his fingers to his hat and smiled brightly back at her. It was one of those smiles guys gave when they were totally sunk for a girl, but Chris figured the guy had to be at least ten years her senior.

The balding cop tapped her open window. "You'd best get going, JD—and did you have a chance to talk to your mother yet?"

Chris found himself watching the younger cop. What was his name, Ray? He stood there, no longer worried about Chris because he seemed to have eyes only for the babe in the car. He wondered whether Daddy had any idea his partner had the hots for his daughter. At the same time, he realized neither of them was giving him the time of day now. Could he just pick up his wrecked helmet, climb on his bike, and drive away? Likely not, considering they still had his license and registration, and his gear, which had been tied to the back but was now tossed by the side of the road.

He didn't hear what she said, but then the car started moving, rolling the ten feet toward him, where it stopped, the passenger window still open. "Hey there, don't let these two ruffle your feathers. They're both harmless…and should know better than to pull over a stranger just because!" She yelled the last part back, looking over her shoulder.

Chris took in the pair he'd been shitting bricks about moments before, who now appeared a lot less threatening.

"You should stop in Martin on your way through. Come on over to Lulu's. Dinner is on the house for your trouble. The name's JD," she added with that killer smile, and he could see her killer body, too, where she sat in the bucket seat behind the wheel. She was wearing a floral tank and cutoffs. Then she lifted her fingers in a wave as she pulled away, and he stared at the back end of the car and then back to the cops, who still hadn't told him why they'd felt the need to scare the ever-living shit out of him and treat him like America's most wanted.

"Here's your ID," said Ray, the scowl now once again pasted on his face. He held out Chris's papers and license.

Chris ripped them from the cop's hand, biting back a few choice words that would've likely had him cuffed again, face down on the burning blacktop.

The older cop, who was already walking to the passenger side of the cop car, where the lights were still flashing, lifted his hand. "You have yourself a great day, you hear, and move yourself along."

Chris would've been a fool to miss the warning in his tone. Then they were both in the car, and as it drove away with one blast of the siren, he noted the logo on its side, *Bennett County Sheriff's Department.*

He tucked his ID back in its compartment along with his wallet and things, then leaned down and picked up his helmet, taking in the crack right down the center of the visor. The repairs would be a pain in the ass to see through. The helmet was a big-ticket item, and he wasn't too happy to dish out that kind of cash. He wanted nothing more than to give those two asshole cops the bill and make them pay it. *Yeah, good luck there.*

At least now he knew where he was: South Dakota, outside Martin, in the middle of nowhere. Then there was the gorgeous chick, the daughter of the asshole older cop who'd pulled him over, and he realized maybe he wasn't too willing to listen to their advice. After all, as his mom and dad had pointed out a time or two, there was a side of Chris that just couldn't resist stirring up trouble, challenging authority, going toe to toe, when the smarter course would be to walk away.

He stared at the crack in his visor, his gear on the ground, and figured, why not? Dinner sounded like one hell of a great idea.

Chapter Two

Locals liked to tease JD that if she were ever open to getting married, she'd have a line of suitors around the block. But then, every one of those locals had conveniently forgotten the fact that she had already been married once, even if it had been for only five minutes at the age of seventeen. As her father had pointed out, it had been a split second of rebellious teenage stupidity, her one and only folly.

If only everyone knew the truth of the matter.

Now she was stuck here even though said moment of stupidity had stirred a spark, the possibility of getting away from this small town and into a life she wanted to create for herself—not that she had any idea of what that looked like or could be.

"I was down at Fielding Foods, and the ground beef was marked down to half price, so I picked up thirty pounds," her mother said. "Figured we could fill the freezer and do a special next week on meatloaf."

Alice Cayhill was a former beauty queen and had been the runner-up in the state pageant just over twenty years earlier. She was slender and curvy, with honey-brown hair. JD favored her mother, something else the townsfolk liked to point out. She should've been flattered, especially considering her mother could still turn a man's eye, but then, said men would have to deal with her father, the sheriff of Martin, where nothing ever happened and no one ever dared to cross him.

It wasn't so much that he was a bad man. Jorden Cayhill was a teddy bear to those who knew him, namely his family, but at the same time, he didn't take to anyone messing with them. Hence JD's short-lived marriage and the fact that she was now the head cook and baker at the Cayhills' one-hundred-year-old family lodge.

"JD, didn't you hear me?" her mom said, now looking into the open freezer. She reached for a plastic bag on the counter.

"Sorry, was just…" JD lifted her hands. One was holding a potato peeler, the other a half-peeled potato. She stood over the extra-large farmhouse sink, where she'd been staring off out the window, thinking about what could have been.

"Daydreaming again? Lord, I'd love to know what's going through that mind of yours." Her mother tossed the bag into the freezer and shut the door. "But I was just saying that I can handle the deliveries tomorrow for the shut-ins. I think we're up to almost twenty this week. Saw the orders. I swear this town has more elderly and less young. Just last week the Croftons' eldest got a job out in Cleveland, packed his young family up, and moved away. We just don't seem to be attracting any of that young family blood. The school here is going to be in real trouble if any more of our young ones up and move off. We'll be left with the old, the really old, and then just us, and that…"

Her mom was in the dining room now, still talking, but JD couldn't make out anything else she was saying. It was always the same; her mom talked just to talk. JD and her dad had learned to smile and nod at all the right times, though she swore her dad never heard a word her mother said. She wondered when or whether her mother would ever figure that part out.

"JD, there's a young man here asking for you," her mom said as she hurried back from the front, her amber eyes popping. "Never seen him before. Rode in on one of those big noisy bikes." As if he could hear her, she lowered her voice, whispering loudly and dramatically. "He looks like one of those biker guys. A very attractive one, at that. You got something you want to tell me, like why he'd be asking for you?"

She had to think for a minute, as she didn't have a clue what her mom was talking about. She dropped the potato and peeler into the sink and then wiped her hands on a dish towel as she strode to the open door, where she took in someone tall, handsome, and redheaded.

Holy shit! She froze for a second as her stomach zigged, her hands slapping the doorframe. She felt beads of sweat under her arms. Her mom bumped into her as she stared at the biker her father had cuffed face down on the scorching blacktop. Damn, he was even more attractive than she'd realized.

And, of course, what was that hot biker doing but watching her with what she thought were the most vibrant blue eyes she'd ever seen? She was also getting a very real firsthand view of all his fine assets, from his height to his broad shoulders and chest. A flicker of amusement seemed to dance in his expression, and even the hint of a smile that touched his lips had her knees softening in horror. She was sure her mom was reading her reaction. She could feel her face heat.

"Where, again, did you meet him?" her mother whispered in her ear, loudly. Of course he heard. She wanted to shoo her away, flicking her hand toward her.

"Hi, uh…" JD started, feeling out of her depth, sounding like an idiot, she was sure. She'd never expected to see him again, not after the welcome he'd been on the receiving end of on that deserted highway from her father and Ray.

"JD, right? Chris Friessen. Guess we didn't get to meet properly." He walked toward her, wearing a black leather jacket and black pants, the kind guys wore to ride motorbikes, with his helmet tucked under his arm. Something about him ratcheted up the tension in the room. "I can tell by your expression that you completely forgot about your offer."

She wondered whether her mouth gaped.

Her mom whispered loudly in her ear, "What offer?" Her tone was one of pure shock, accusing, as JD turned to see her very dramatic expression.

She stepped away from the open door and over to Chris. She had to look up, and oh, wow, was he tall. She stood about five foot five, and her head just barely topped his shoulders. She couldn't remember ever having seen someone with such vibrant red hair. He really was smoking hot, the total package. The hand he was now holding out to her was large, a man's hand, not at all neatly polished. Touching it, she wondered whether he could feel what a wreck she was now.

"Of course, yes," she said. "Sorry, I was just working on dinner and didn't think you'd stop in."

He was still holding her hand as he lifted his gaze over to her mom, and JD finally pulled away from his strong grip. It was the kind of touch that had her wondering indecently what he could do with those hands.

"I offered Chris dinner on the house," JD said, "considering I drove up on Daddy and Ray cuffing him face down on the burning pavement. They said it was just a routine traffic stop when I asked, but you know Daddy. How long would he have toyed with him if I hadn't driven up and said something?"

Her mom crossed her arms. "Mm-hmm," she said, a bit of amusement in her eyes. Then she did that hair flick thing she did when openly flirting with an attractive man before sweeping her hand in the air as if it was nothing. "Jorden is just a big old teddy bear and wouldn't hurt anyone, but he's real quick to make sure certain types don't even think about stopping and visiting—you know, the kind of people who don't belong here, slickers in their overpriced sports cars, bikers, and anyone up to no good. Sorry, it's just his way. He doesn't mean anything by it. He's just protecting the community here, which is one of the safest anywhere, the kind of place…"

Her mother could go on and on, so she reached over and touched her arm. "Mom, I think I heard the phone ringing a moment ago," she said, pointing to the front of the house. Even Chris turned to look behind him at the ancient long front desk made of dark wood and brass.

"You sure? I didn't hear anything."

"Mom, you should check. I don't think anyone is booked in tonight, but that could be someone looking…" She let the words fall away, knowing her mom always needed to know what was going on with the lodge, sticking her nose in the running of everything even though everyone was looking after what needed to be looked after.

"You're right. I should," Alice said and tapped her wrist, then started walking. But she stopped right beside

Chris, letting her hand touch his arm and the leather of his jacket. JD wanted to cringe in embarrassment, as her mom also made a flirty sound of approval as she allowed her gaze to linger a little too long. Then she was gone, and that left JD with Mister Hotty, who was watching her mom walk away. He seriously had to be considering the wisdom of staying now.

"I did promise you dinner on the house, didn't I?" she said. Now she had all his attention.

"You did, at that. When you said Lulu's, I wasn't expecting this." He was looking around, and she wondered what he was really seeing behind the quaint, rustic charm. The dining room held five tables, all mismatched, which added to the old-time feel. "It's the type of place I've been looking for in my travels, seeing this country and all its charm."

"I hope you're not disappointed in any way. Come in. I'll get you to a table, and, as you can see, you have your choice. We're not particularly busy right now, just the locals who come in for the dinner rush at five. You are early…" It was only three thirty, and she still hadn't finished prepping that night's menu. She had work to do, yet there was a man she wondered so many things about.

"Not too early, I hope."

She shook her head and tossed him an easy smile as she walked over to a table by the window. "Not at all."

He was right on her heels, and she could feel his heat, hearing the floorboards creak. She glanced back to him as he said, "Good to hear. The way things have worked out, this'll be kind of a late lunch, early dinner." Then he settled his megawatt gaze on her. That one look had her rooted where she stood, not wanting to move, feeling the air between them sizzle. She was glad her mom had left. "So what's good here?" he asked, and the way he was staring at her, the way he angled his head for a moment, she thought there was a deeper meaning hidden in the question.

"Ah, everything, considering I'm the cook," she said, wondering why she'd added that last part.

"So not only do I get the pleasure of seeing you again, but I get to have you cook for me."

The air sizzled, and she found herself sliding her hand around the back of her neck and lifting her hair to cool off. The room was warm. The windows were cracked, but it wasn't the heat of the day that was making her a little crazy.

She took in the edge of his smile. It seemed he was openly and shamelessly flirting with her, and for a moment she felt as if he could see right through everything she was wearing, as if he was picturing her naked. Danger seemed to ripple in the chemistry that sizzled between them.

She should walk away.

"You said you were traveling?" She thought her voice sounded a little deep and sexy. That wasn't like her, but it was at this moment. What was it about this hot biker that was bringing out the siren inside her? She touched the side of her head and then dragged her hand over the back of her neck again.

"Yeah, seeing this beautiful country, all the backroads and small towns in half the states." He was still smiling, and not just from his mouth. He was giving everything to her in that one look. How was it that a guy could do that?

"Wow, that sounds amazing. How long have you been traveling? I just can't imagine being able to do something like that." It sounded crazy, but it also sounded like heaven, something her father would never allow.

"A few months. Saved up and planned for it. Was something I always dreamed of doing before I decide on what to do, where to settle down and how. It seemed seeing this country when I'm young, with no one to depend on me, is better than waiting like most people do for when they retire. So I worked, socked everything away, and planned out the key places and states."

She realized they were still standing, and she glanced at the table for four by the window and gestured to it. "Where're my manners? Here, why don't you have a seat?" She could get lost in everything about him. She thought she could talk to him all night. What was it about his charm? It oozed from every part of him without him saying one word.

She was in so much trouble.

"Only if you'll join me," he said, then stepped around her and pulled out a chair.

"Well, for a minute, but then I have to get dinner on or you won't be eating anything." She sat down, and he pushed the chair in and walked around the table to the seat across from her. There was an echo in the empty room, she realized, and a peace that seemed to exist only when no one was there.

"I can wait, but I'm enjoying the conversation. You know, meeting new folks is also a part of seeing this country." It wasn't lost on her how he filled that old wooden chair. He rested his motorcycle helmet on the table beside him, and she took in the cracked visor.

"That had to have hurt." She gestured toward it, and she wasn't sure what she saw in his expression as he glanced to it and back to her, the smile gone.

"So, Lulu's, how long have you worked here?" he said.

She realized he hadn't answered her. She wondered whether he had any idea how annoying that was. There was something about the way he spoke, his voice, that had her staring at his face, his expression, his full lips.

"It's the family business, so I grew up here, lived here. This lodge has been in our family for generations, ever since my great-great-grandfather moved out here and started it up mostly for travelers heading west. There were rooms upstairs and a restaurant down, but now there're just three rooms up there. The back of the lodge is an addition from a decade ago for the family. I just kind of was always in the kitchen, helping, and now…" She lifted her hands.

She couldn't remember the exact day she'd started doing all the cooking, all the baking. It had been after her grandmother announced she was retiring two years earlier. Grandma Cayhill had taken off her apron, tossed it down, and said she was passing it on. Then she and JD's grandfather had moved to a house a block away, where they now had a social life that occupied their every waking moment.

"Family business, heritage, pretty cool," he said. "Just the kind of mom and pop place I was looking for. So you still rent out rooms?"

She pulled in a breath. "We do," she said.

She heard the door and glanced around Chris to see Ray stepping inside. He lifted off his shades, his intense gaze going right to her, with that smile he had for her every time she saw him. That was until he spotted Chris. It was instant, the change in him. He took a step into the lodge and closed the door behind him, then took one step, two steps, before his gaze locked on Chris and shifted to something dark, something she hadn't seen in his expression before.

"Hey, Ray, wasn't expecting you so soon," she said without getting up. She noted the way Chris leaned back in the chair, which creaked under his weight, as if getting ready for…what? The way he stared right back at Ray, it seemed he was unimpressed. Angry, maybe? Whatever this was between them, they seemed like two bulls in a field, ready to go at each other.

Ray dragged his gaze to JD for a second but then went right back to Chris. He stood right in front of him, dialing up the tension in the room. His hands settled on his belt, close to his gun, his cuffs. Then he flicked his hand to Chris. "Now what, exactly, are you doing here?"

Chris stared up at him, far from rattled. In fact, he crossed his arms as if enjoying the moment. "Well, I was invited," he said without pulling his gaze from Ray. He wasn't intimidated at all. Then he looked over to JD, settling his megawatt gaze on her completely, and jutted his chin toward her. "As a matter of fact, though, I was just about to ask JD out. So how about it?"

She stared at him in horror. Was he toying with her? "How about what?" she said. Her mom was now walking their way, and her dad had just come in, too. This was quickly going sideways.

Chris pulled in a breath. "Going out with me. After dinner, when you're off, I'll take you out, just you and me."

All she could do was take in the way Ray was shaking his head, as if he had some say in the matter. She realized the spotlight was shining on her. "You know what, Chris? I would love to go out with you," she announced.

"What?" Ray snapped, taking a step closer to her.

Her mom and dad were staring at her as if she'd lost her mind. She'd toed the line for too long now, yet there was something about this badass guy. Chris exuded the kind of charm she couldn't remember ever feeling from a guy before.

Chapter Three

"She's spoken for," Ray said.

Chris was staring into the face of one pissed-off officer, or was he a deputy? He couldn't quite tell from the badge pinned to his chest. The dark-haired cop was now seated across from him in the rustic dining room of the quaint lodge, in the exact spot in which JD had been sitting just moments earlier.

Chris glanced over his shoulder to the door that led into what he thought was the kitchen, which was still swinging from where JD had been pulled away by her mother. Her father, the sheriff, had paused a second to level him a look that said, *What the fuck do you think you're doing, boy?* before following the women into the kitchen. It wasn't lost on Chris how gorgeous JD was. With her amazing figure, her sexy curves, he could've watched her all day. He could see clearly who she took after in looks.

He allowed his eyes to scan the room, taking his time before looking back to Ray, who had to have at least ten years, if not more, he figured, on JD. "Didn't seem that way to me," he said. He knew he was playing with fire but just couldn't help himself in wanting to stir up trouble and push the small-town cop.

He was well aware how badly this could go for him, especially since his family didn't know exactly where he was today, but then, Chris had never been known to follow the rules or play it safe. Hence his bike and this little cross-country adventure, and the fact he was messing with someone who could seriously cause him a world of trouble.

"Well, now you know," Ray said. His hands were big, and the one on the table flicked to him as he relaxed in the chair. Chris wasn't fooled for a second into thinking the man wasn't waiting for him to move or do something he wouldn't like. He wondered at what point he'd find himself cuffed again, maybe with a gun in his face, all because he wasn't about to cower under this prick. "So it'd be best if you moved on now."

Chris actually laughed. "Yeah, that doesn't really work for me. You see, I was invited here and offered dinner, and that's exactly what I plan to have. Then I have plans after with the lady. I keep my word, too. Not really the kind of man to ask a lady out and then take off. That would be rude, Ray."

He knew he was provoking the man, the way he tossed back his own attitude. The cop was staring at him, his icy blue eyes flashing. The temperature had dropped to near frigid. Chris knew pushing any cop was just a bad idea, period, but he couldn't stop himself.

Ray let out a rough laugh, the kind of laugh that dragged an icy chill down Chris's spine. He had to fight the urge to look away. But he wasn't about to cower under this asshole, who was doing his best to grind him into the ground. "That's chief deputy to you, asshole," Ray said, then winked. "And as I said, JD is not for you. She's been spoken for, so you just get back on your bike, ride on out of our county, and keep going back to where you came from." He nodded then as if it was all settled, but Chris had no intention of leaving.

"You keep saying that, spoken for. What does that mean, exactly? By you?" He eased back in the chair, hearing it creak. His leather jacket was making him sweat. He should have taken a moment to take it off, but not now, as the man across from him had every intention of keeping him from seeing JD. If he were smart, he'd have made his excuses and left. Good thing he wasn't that cowardly.

"It's not your business…" Ray started, but the sound of the kitchen door opening had him stopping midsentence.

"So sorry about that, Chris," JD said. "I brought you an iced tea, not that I asked you what you'd like to drink." She rested a tall glass complete with ice and a mint leaf on top in front of him, and he did his best to ignore the deputy seated across from him, who was staring at JD like a man in love. What was the story there?

"Ray, are you behaving yourself, or are you trying to intimidate Chris again?" JD added as she set a menu in front of him. It was just a single page with four items to choose from: a blue-plate dinner special, chili, steak, and the staple of every restaurant around, a house burger.

"I'm doing no such thing, but, JD, you don't know nothing about this man here. Inviting him for dinner and then saying you'll go out with him? No, that's not right. I'm sure your dad in there was likely telling you…"

She held up the flat of her hand, and he stopped talking. She rested both her hands on her hips, outfitted in a loose pair of jeans. She had one of the nicest asses Chris had ever seen, and with her long legs and slim waist, she was the entire package. Chris was in no hurry to walk out of there. Cop dad or not, there was something about JD that intrigued him so much that he thought it would be well worth a moment of his time and this minor discomfort to get to know her.

"Ray Briggs," she said, "you know very well that no one tells me what to do, and that includes my parents. I'm of age and can make my own decisions, and I've invited Chris for dinner—and, just so everyone is clear, after the dinner rush, I'll also be going out with him. So you're welcome to move on over to another table and take a seat, or if Chris is fine with you sharing his table, I'll take your order in just a moment."

His interest was piqued even more, and he found himself taking in the deputy, who was staring up at her with what resembled puppy dog eyes. Clearly, the infatuation was one sided, but the fact was that he was head over heels in love with her. What the hell was he walking into?

"Ah, come on, JD," Ray said. "I was planning on taking you out. We'd go park up on Slater's Hill and watch the sunset."

Even Chris gave him a look that said, *Seriously, dude?*

JD was shaking her head, and he wondered whether she had any idea how Ray had set his sights on her. "Sorry. Now, are you going to behave yourself here, or do I need to move you to another table?" she said. JD could make that deputy asshole toe the line, Chris realized, or maybe that was just the effect she had on men. Then she gave him that sassy expression, the same one she had given him through her open passenger window. It was beyond gorgeous and had him sunk. There was no way he was walking away now. "So, Chris, what can I get you for dinner?"

"Well, I'm thinking, why don't you surprise me?" He lifted the menu and handed it back to her.

For a moment, she seemed rattled, but then she gave her head a shake and pasted a smile back on her face. "Okay, one blue-plate special." Her gaze lingered a minute before turning to Ray. "And how about you, Ray? What would you like tonight?"

He had both hands clasped over his belt as he leaned back. "The same," he said, inclining his head to Chris, "and be sure to hold back a piece of your apple pie. I'll be wanting that for dessert."

She gave him a nod before turning over a cup. "Coffee then, too," she added as she walked over to an antique buffet, where a coffee station was set up. She strode back, and he noticed the flip flops on her feet.

"I do, just the way you make it," Ray said.

She poured him a coffee and set two creamers beside the cup. As she walked away, Ray dumped both in his coffee and stirred before tapping the spoon against his mug. Chris didn't miss the fact that the cop was still sitting at his table, the last person he'd ever have wanted to share a meal with, and was now staring at him. Chris was smart enough to know that every man had a breaking point, and by the look in his eyes, Ray was evidently close to his. So JD was his trigger.

"If you hurt her or mess with her in any way, I will kill you and bury you where no one will ever find you," Ray said. He kept his voice low, but his meaning was clear. "So have your dinner. You want to take her out? You be sure she returns safely, early, and you don't mess with her in any way." Then he lifted his coffee and jabbed his finger over to Chris. "You just remember who her father is. She belongs here, and if you step out of line in any way…" He stopped talking and shook his head so slowly. "I'm watching you."

Now what the hell was he supposed to say to that? Nothing, if he was smart. He lifted the iced tea and took a swallow, tasting the sweetness, then flicked his gaze over to the deputy and said, "So how long have you been in love with her?"

Chapter Four

W ho would have thought that tonight, of all nights, would be the night that every person in town, or so it seemed, would show up for the dinner rush? Her mom and dad had both pitched in and carried out plates as she dished up the orders, and even Ray had stepped into the kitchen a time or two to help out their only waitress, Sue, a single mother of three, who worked four nights a week or as needed. Word had gotten out that the blue-plate special was grilled pork chops with steamed carrots over creamy whipped mashed potatoes, gravy, and buttermilk biscuits. JD would have to make a note of the favorites and time it better.

As she stared at the stacks of dirty plates and pots, she wanted to weep with weariness. It had to be after eight now, and her feet were killing her.

"Well, that young man is still here," Alice said, "and you should know that your dad and Ray are both out there, breathing down his neck. He says he's not leaving, that he asked you out and intends on taking you out. Never seen anyone so persistent. Not sure if that boy is just plain stupid or if he has more grit than is good for him."

JD just stared at her mother in horror. How could she have forgotten? She pulled off her apron, wanting to change, feeling the dampness of sweat seeping through her tank top. "He's still here? Why didn't you say something? I completely forgot."

Her mother reached for the apron she had taken off, and JD realized she was no longer horrified at the fact that a biker no one knew anything about had not only shown up for the dinner she'd offered but also asked her out. That was despite the fact that her father had stood in front of her in the kitchen a few hours ago, telling her in no uncertain terms that she could go out with Chris only over his dead body.

Now here she was, sweaty and gritty, wanting to take a shower and get off her feet, not go out on a date or on the town or anywhere except to bed. But pride was pride, and she damn sure was done being dictated to.

"Well, I'm saying something now," Alice said. "Are you sure you know what you're doing? I mean, you know nothing about him, where he's from, or who his people are. He's not from here, JD. Going out with someone not from Martin lacks wisdom. And don't forget there's Ray. You know he's not happy about you going out with him."

Her mom was so dramatic about everything. She wanted to roll her eyes. It was all she'd ever heard, growing up, as if anyone not from Martin was from another country. It was as if everything and everyone that mattered was right there, and any other place didn't exist. Then there was Ray.

"Mom, hate to break this to you, but Chris is just like you and me. We're all the same people. And yes, I'm going out with him." Where, she didn't have a clue, but right now she wasn't about to waste another minute being questioned by her parents. "And about Ray, I'm going to say this one last time: He has no say in my life, in who I see or talk to," she added.

Her mother leveled her with one of her disapproving looks before giving her head a shake, knowing she wasn't changing JD's mind. "You know Ray has been stopping in here every night and has intentions of asking you out. He's already spoken to your father…"

JD wanted to bang her head against the wall, but she let out a sigh instead. It was always the same, the nudge toward Ray. Of course she knew Ray was interested, yet he'd never even kissed her. He'd taken her out a few times, walking, to a movie, even dancing a time or two, but as far as she was concerned, they were friends. He'd listened to her, being the sympathetic ear when her father had pulled her and Matt apart and ended any future they could have had.

"Mom, Ray is just a friend. How many times have I said that? He's nothing more, never has been, never will be. So can you please stop, already? Both you and Daddy need to learn that my life is my life. I decide, not you."

There it was, the eye roll again, as if she were spouting nonsense. It seemed her parents would never see her as an adult with a life that was hers alone. And worse, she realized she would never be free of them continually poking their noses into her business and arranging her life as they saw fit.

So she turned away and pushed open the kitchen door. Three sets of eyes turned her way. Ray and her dad were both standing in front of Chris, their arms crossed, and it wasn't lost on her that they were roughly the same height, neither towering over the other. Then there was Chris, who must have been staring right back at them, his arms also crossed over a rust-colored T-shirt. She noticed he'd shed his leather jacket, and wow, his arms showed he was a man who could hold his own. Maybe that was why he was standing up to Ray and her dad as if it were no big deal. That alone bumped him up a double notch in her book.

"You ready?" he said as he turned and walked her way.

She didn't dare look over to her father, because she already knew he likely had a few things to say, and she wasn't about to hear any more of his demands and carrying on about how she could or couldn't do something. "Yes, just let me change into a clean shirt and we can go," she said.

Then she did slide her gaze over to her father and Ray before glancing back to Chris, wondering how much longer he could hold them off. "You okay here?" she said, gesturing over to her dad and Ray. There had to be a point where he realized she was too much trouble and walked out. Anyone in his right mind would have. Wasn't that what Matt had done?

He shrugged as if it were no big deal. "Of course. Go get changed. I'll be here," he said.

She took another step back, taking in her dad and Ray, and hesitated. "You two, behave yourselves," she added with a dash of annoyance to hopefully drive her point home. Then she turned, glancing back only once to see her mom step out of the kitchen and over to Chris with that flirty smile that could bring a world of trouble.

All JD could think was *Good grief.* She hoped her mom, at least, would behave.

∼

JD DIDN'T LINGER in her bedroom as she wanted even though she wished for a few minutes to climb in the shower. Instead, she kicked off her flip flops, pulled off her damp and sweaty shirt, and stepped out of her jeans. She tossed both in her dirty clothes hamper, taking in her queen bed, neatly made with a green floral quilt, a night stand, a chest of drawers that was as old as the house, and two antique chairs in front of a fireplace that didn't work.

She crossed into her private bathroom, with its claw-foot tub and single sink, and turned on the tap to splash water on her underarms and over her face. She grabbed the towel, taking a whiff to make sure she didn't smell, and dried off before putting on deodorant.

She pulled a clean pair of jeans from her drawer and stepped barefoot into them, then reached for a deep blue frilly tank from her closet, which she pulled on over a black lacy bra. She grabbed silver hoops from the square box on her dresser and put them on, glancing at her image in the bathroom mirror. Not bad, considering she'd been sweating over a hot stove for hours.

She quickly added blusher to her cheeks and then a thin coat of mascara before giving a quick glance to the clock, seeing that only five minutes had passed. "Good girl." She wanted to pat herself on the back, still feeling the urgency as she took in her shoe rack and shoved her feet into a dressier pair of black toeless sandals.

She was out the door, half expecting Chris to be gone this time, but she froze when she saw her mother behind the ancient front desk and Chris filling out a registration card. They both looked up and over to her as if what they were doing was completely normal.

"Since it's getting late, I suggested that Chris get a room for the night," Alice said. "No point in him having to hit the highway in the dark." She slid a key across the counter. "5C, the first door at the top of the stairs."

Chris pulled out his wallet and tossed several bills down. "Thank you," he said and took the key, which scraped across the counter. He dragged those mesmerizing blue eyes, which she could totally get lost in, from her mom to her. "You ready?"

She found herself looking over her shoulder into the dining room, expecting to see Ray and her dad there, but she saw no one, instead hearing a clatter from the kitchen. "Sure," was all she said.

"Well, you two have fun," Alice added with that flirty smile. "I'd best go give Sue help cleaning up." Then her mother did the oddest thing: She walked away, leaving Chris and JD alone.

"Your mom…" He gestured to her retreating back. "You look just like her."

She dragged her gaze back to him, taking in the leather biking pants he was still wearing, and wondered what to make of the comment.

"You mind if I grab my gear and put it in my room? And I'll take off these bike leathers," he said, tapping his leg.

"Of course not. Was wondering whether you'd wear those all night. You have to be hot, I would think," she added.

Chris pulled open the front door. The jingle of the bell was as familiar as the night sky, and he waited for her to step through it, the trait of a gentleman, another plus in his favor. "I am hot, but it's a safety thing on a bike. They won't protect against broken bones, but they will against road rash."

He was behind her as she stepped out of the lodge. The sun was still up, but it was starting to dip lower. It really was magical out there when the sun went down. She watched as Chris pulled the door closed, and then they started down the four long steps together, side by side, the wood creaking under his weight. His bike was parked right in front beside her father's cruiser. It really was a nice bike, as far as motorcycles went.

He said nothing as he strode ahead of her and unfastened the bag on the back, and she took a moment to really look at him. She couldn't put her finger on what it was that oozed from him, a kind of alpha charm that was different from any man she'd met before. It left her feeling uneasy. She could feel herself easily slipping into something that could leave her silently dying inside when he pulled away and left this town.

"So you've traveled all over on this bike?" She stepped off the curb and ran her hand over the metal and onto the leather seat, looking at the bike, not at him.

"I did, the only way to see the country." He hefted the bag over his shoulder.

She couldn't fight the need to really look at him as he waited for her. A smile touched his lips, and his intense blue eyes didn't look away. All that accomplished was to make her feel as if she were special in a way no man ever had, not even Matt. Then he was walking back to the steps, and he paused as if waiting for her to fall in beside him. She didn't move for a second as she considered, stay there or go with him?

"So you want to show me the way to 5C," he said, "or do you think your father is waiting in the room for me?"

She hadn't expected that from him. For a second, she wasn't sure whether he was kidding, but she realized that was exactly what her father would do. Maybe that was why she winced and said, "Sure I can. Should I apologize again for my father and Ray? Or maybe I never apologized."

She made herself take a step over to him until she stood right beside him, so close she could feel his heat.

The way he was looking at her now, she wasn't sure what he was thinking. Then he ran his hand over her arm and down to her fingers, a touch that sent a shiver through her. His hand was hard, rough, and warm, and her body seemed to want it. "You don't need to apologize for anyone, JD. Whatever happened, whatever they've done, that's not on you."

He was still holding her hand as they started up the steps, where he opened the front door of the lodge. It was easy with Chris, and maybe that was why she could feel the smile pulling at her lips.

Then there was Ray, waiting behind the front desk, and his eyes went right to their hands before landing solely on her. It felt so much like a punch right in the stomach and left her feeling guilty…over what? She didn't have a clue.

"You know what, Chis?" she said. "Go get changed, and I'll wait right here." She pulled her hand from his and slid it over his arm, feeling his triceps tense with strength.

He glanced over to Ray and then pulled his questioning gaze back to her. "You sure?"

Those two words, the way he said them, she realized he really meant it. Maybe that was why a lump jammed in her throat, cutting off her voice. She had to swallow as she stared into the intensity of his eyes. He had her wanting to step closer to him. What the hell was wrong with her? She didn't behave like this with anyone.

"It's fine." She forced a smile to her lips, dropped her hand, and squeezed her fist from wanting to touch him again.

He nodded, lingering a second more, before starting up the steps to where the three guest rooms were. JD watched him, pulling in one breath and then another, before forcing her gaze back to Ray—who, by the way he was staring at her as he stepped around the front desk toward her, apparently had something on his mind.

One thing she knew well about Ray was that he could be kind and attentive. But he was the same kind of man as her father, one who was evidently determined to have his say.

"So let's have it," JD said, lifting her hands with emphasis as she took a seat on the old-fashioned settee, which was covered in vibrant green velvet. At least her feet were thanking her, and she hoped her face didn't betray the relief she felt.

"Not saying anything, JD. You're a grown woman who's entitled to make her own decisions," Ray said. His blue eyes were more of a steely gray that lacked the brilliance of Chris's, but at the same time, Ray had been the one there on the sidelines when it seemed her life had fallen apart. He'd listened, sympathized, and provided a much needed shoulder to cry on. He'd been the best friend she'd ever had. "But what exactly do you know about him?" he finally said. His expression appeared suddenly cross, annoyed, and for a moment she was at a loss for words.

What was she supposed to say? "I know he hasn't let you and Daddy run him off, scare him away, that he hasn't caved under all the intimidation you've heaped on him since he hit the county line." She crossed her arms and saw the moment her words had an impact.

He flushed for a second before pulling it together. "Point taken. So he's made of stronger stuff—although there is a point for every man, and every man gets there. It's just a matter of finding that weak spot," he stated as he stepped closer to her. He stopped just in front of her, and she was forced to look up. Ray's dark hair was wavy, a little on the messy side, and she didn't need to remind herself that his build was a fine thing to look at. She'd been pulled into those strong arms and held a few times as she'd cried into his chest. She'd been comforted there and knew how good a place it was, how it felt. She had to blink away the memory, reminding herself he was a friend. A good friend.

"I seriously hope that isn't your way of saying you're about to pull out all the stops with him and maybe take things a little further with the intimidation, bullying. I don't think I want to know what else you and my father are willing to stoop to," she stated.

Ray had the grace to glance away as if thinking of what to say, or maybe he was running a little thin on excuses and was deciding whether to keep his plans for Chris from her or share them. She was well aware of how the law in Martin seemed to do what it wanted for the good of the community. It always had.

"I'm going to say it again, JD: He's not for you. You know nothing about him, just a no-good drifter who'll be gone tomorrow, and then what?" He slid his hand under her chin, then tilted it up so she had to look at him and see the caring he had for her. Damn, that hurt.

"Oh, for Pete's sake," she said. "Would you and everyone stop this? Chris just asked me out. You're all acting as if this was a marriage proposal." She swatted his hand away and shook her head.

He placed both hands over his belt, where his gun was holstered alongside the pouch where he kept his cuffs—a cop who was always ready. "Well, that's the thing, JD. I remember not so long ago that you were sweet-talked into that very thing, and if I recall, it didn't work out so well for you. If you need a reminder of how low you were and who was there for you…" he said, but she didn't need a reminder of the moment she'd seen the papers with Matt's signature and the note that he was gone.

"Of course I remember." She pulled her arms closer, crossing them under her breasts, feeling the giant ache that had taken a chunk out of her heart. She knew that Ray had been there, letting her cry it out away from everyone's prying eyes. He'd been a shield from everyone and the world when she'd needed it. Apparently, he wasn't going to let her forget that.

There was a creak, and Ray turned and stepped back. She looked up as Chris stepped off the last step, wearing blue jeans and a dark blue T-shirt, his hair a little damp as if he'd taken a second to clean up. Then he was looking from her to Ray, his expression telling her he'd heard something. He seemed questioning, confused. He said nothing as he stood there, staring at Ray, and the look in his eyes let her know he would push at Ray until he either snapped or pushed back. They were two alphas, neither about to be jerked around by the other, the kind of guys who won or ended things badly.

JD slapped her hands on her thighs and stood. "Well, I see you're ready and had time to change. That's great. We should go." Even she didn't miss how direct her tone was.

Maybe that was all Chris needed, because he pulled his gaze from Ray. His smile for her was long gone. Now there was just a hard and unforgiving expression for the cop who had messed with him.

As he took a step toward JD, however, something in his expression softened for her. He slid his hand over her shoulder and down her back, a possessive move. She would've had to be a fool to miss the pissing contest between Chris and Ray. For a reason she couldn't explain, she was the trophy they were vying for. He reached around her for the door and pulled it open.

"JD," Ray said.

She froze, feeling Chris's hand running over her shoulder now. She turned back to Ray but said nothing, whereas the look on his face said everything.

"You need me for anything, I'm just a call away," he said. It was the caring in his voice that bothered her, so she turned away and stepped out onto the front porch, then heard the door close behind her.

She stopped when Chris pulled his hand away and glanced up to him, wondering what he was thinking. He still wasn't smiling.

"Seems as if I've walked into the middle of something," he said. "I'm now wondering whether maybe this is more than I bargained for."

For a second, she felt her heart dip.

"There's only one thing I want to know," he added as she forced herself to swallow past the dryness in her throat.

"And that is?" she said, then waited.

He nodded and glanced into the distance before dragging his gaze back to her. "Is there anything going on between you and the deputy that I should know about?" He jammed his thumb to the door.

She could see it then: He was questioning the wisdom of staying, and all his charm had been neatly pulled back and tucked away, as if he indeed had something to protect. "Ray and I are not involved. We're friends, that's all. I'm not involved with anyone or seeing anyone, and if I were, I wouldn't have accepted your invite to go out. I'm single, unattached, but maybe I should be asking you if this is just a game between you and Ray. Maybe some hard feelings linger, or is this about taking me out just to push his buttons? Chris, are you interested in taking me out?"

Please say yes. She wanted him to, but she feared he'd come to his senses, shake his head, and decide to get on his bike and leave town. If he was smart, he would. She hoped he wasn't.

He looked up the street and then over to her. "I guess I have my answer then. Yes, I want to take you out, and since I'm not familiar with this place and what there is to do around here, I suppose you could show me around." There was that smile that made her feel so good. "Come on," he said, his hand skimming over her lower back as they went down the stairs.

She took in his bike and the street that ran east and west. "Well, how about we walk and I show you all the finer points of Martin?" she said. The lodge was at the center of town, and she started walking down the sidewalk, Chris right beside her, so close his arm was brushing hers.

"So, Chris, since this has been kind of an unusual way to meet, maybe you could tell me where you're from. You said you're traveling. I'd like to hear about it." She was dying to hear about it, actually—an adventure, something she'd only dreamed of and couldn't imagine. Something about him made her want to know everything.

"Actually on my way home now," he said. "I'm from a place outside North Lakewood in Washington state. Grew up on a ranch, my dad's place, but I always had this bug, as my mom called it, to travel—and not just any travel. I wanted to see places no one else does, so I worked my butt off after getting out of school, socked money away, bought my bike, and then made a plan. I left home, went through

Oregon, Nevada, Arizona, and crossed over into New Mexico. Made my way across the country from there over to the east for the past three months. Some places have been unforgettable, and I'd go back, but there are others I hope to never see again."

She watched him. The way he said it, she could see there was an experience or something else there, a memory that would likely haunt him, or so it seemed. "But mostly good?" she prompted, wondering what he was holding on to.

He glanced down to her, forced a smile, and nodded. "Mostly good."

"And you don't want to share the bad?" She wondered whether he meant what had happened that day, what she'd driven up on.

Whatever it was, he shook his head. "No, some things aren't worth sharing. That's the problem with this world, I think. Everyone keeps stirring up what's not working and talking it to death, keeping it alive in everyone's minds when it's best to let it go. So no, I won't share the bad." He was being cryptic. This was the first time she'd ever met someone unwilling to share a problem.

"So is today one of those bad things? I mean, when I drove up on you…" She let her words fall away as his expression darkened and his heavy gaze fell on her. What was it about the way he could look at her? She wondered what he was thinking, feeling. Not an easy man, she figured.

He shook his head. "No, that was more an annoyance than anything, but I have to ask, is that a regular occurrence around here?"

What could she say? She suspected it happened more often than not, considering the town didn't see many troublemakers, but she didn't think she'd share that last part.

Seeing a lone biker on a backroad stretch of highway, her dad and Ray would've been wondering what he was up to. She tensed her jaw and felt his hand slide over her lower back and rub before he pulled it away.

"It's okay," he said. "I can see you're having some trouble thinking of what to say, but I think you just answered my question."

"Well, wait." She stopped and stepped in front of him, pressing her hand to his chest, feeling the ripple of muscle, those pecs, solid, strong. She had to pull her hand back because touching him felt too good. "My father isn't a bad man, and neither is Ray. In fact, they care about everyone in this town. They want to see that everyone is safe and make sure it stays that way. Maybe in some of those places you stopped, whatever those experiences were, they wouldn't have happened if those places had people like my father and Ray seeing that everyone was safe and protected."

And sheltered, she thought. Martin was a place where nothing overly exciting happened, but then, there hadn't been a murder in the county in over ten years.

The way he was looking down at her, she wondered what he was thinking. "That's too simplistic an answer, JD. I can see you feel you need to make your dad's case, and the deputy's, but it's not necessary."

She had a feeling he was blowing her off, or rather, he wasn't willing to hear any of her dad's or Ray's good points. "I think it is necessary," she said. "My father wouldn't hurt a fly, and while I'm sure you may have been inconvenienced unnecessarily, I can assure you that was all that would've happened. My father has done so many things to help this community. He was the first one to set up and sponsor meals for the shut-ins, all the elderly, so they can stay in their homes longer instead of being dumped in some nursing homes where they'd be stuffed in a corner, waiting to die. He's on the council of three community organizations that provide food, shelter, and aid to those who need it here. He cares, and so does Ray," she added, wanting him to see her father and Ray the way she did, through the eyes of everyone in Martin, rather than focusing on the flaws she wished he hadn't seen.

"I get it, JD, I do. Seriously, it's not a problem," he said, reaching out and pressing his hand to her shoulder. He squeezed, then gestured behind her. "So how about I take you for a drink?"

She took in where he had gestured, to the flashing sign of the Moose bar and grill. Not much of a place, but at least they could sit and talk, and she could get off her aching feet. And then maybe she could figure out why Chris Friessen had really asked her out.

"Sure, why not?" She shrugged, feeling the unease. She really hoped this wasn't his way of getting back at Ray and her father.

Chapter Six

I t wasn't lost on Chris that half of the buildings in downtown Martin were boarded up. Hard times had evidently hit the area, so why was JD's father steering people away when he should have been welcoming them instead? He wondered what had happened to drive the man to that. It had to have been something, because this didn't make sense, but then, neither did JD, who was sexy and charismatic and hot. Chemistry oozed between them. He couldn't remember having felt an attraction like this before.

He sat on a bar stool at a small table tucked off to the side. JD was sitting across from him, drinking a glass of white wine, a local one that he thought came from a box. He'd chosen draft. Not the best, but it was cold.

"So tell me, JD is short for…?" He left it hanging, and she took a sip of wine and, he thought, had to fight past how bad it was. She said nothing, though, which said a lot about her manners.

"Josephine Denise, but I don't remember anyone ever calling me that. It's quite a mouthful, and I often wonder what my parents were thinking. Me being their only child, I was named after both my grandmothers, so JD has been my name since forever. Never think about it unless I have to fill out some government application or such that calls for all that very specific personal information."

There was something about listening to her talk. She could go on and on if she wanted to, and he thought he could listen to her voice forever. She reached over and pressed her hand over his, which was resting on the table. "What about you? What are your plans for the future? Like what exactly are you going back to in North Lakewood—career, school, girl?"

Oops, there it was. Her brows quirked, and he couldn't stop his laugh as he turned his hand and grasped her fingers, running his thumb over the softness that had created that amazing dinner for him. Even his mom couldn't put out anything that delicious. His mouth watered again as he thought about his first bite of that perfectly cooked chop.

Then he remembered the cop who was completely in love with her.

"No girl, sorry," he said. "Girlfriends aren't made to sit on the sidelines while a guy is off traveling and seeing the country."

He could still picture it as if it were yesterday: His only steady girlfriend, Irene, had hooked up with his best friend, Nick Chambers. He wondered whether he'd ever forget walking in on them naked. Nick had been pounding into her, her legs wrapped around his ass as the bedframe slammed against the wall. "No girlfriends…" He shook his head, pulling his hand away, and lifted his beer.

"I see I've hit a nerve," she said. "Maybe I should offer an apology from all of womankind for whatever she may have done—but then, some women are just as flawed as men."

He took another swallow of his beer. JD didn't seem the type to step out on a guy, or maybe that was just wishful thinking. And he really did think there was more to the story with that deputy, Ray.

"So you had a girlfriend?" she said.

He set his glass down and took in her curiosity.

"But you don't now."

"Something like that."

"Hmm." She sat back and seemed pleased with herself, and a teasing light danced in her eyes. "She left you? You left her?" She narrowed her eyes. "No, she cheated on you." She snapped her fingers as if she'd just solved a mystery. He wasn't sure what tell he had, but her eyes widened and she slapped the top of the table. "She cheated on you, are you kidding? That is…" She actually gestured dramatically as if drawing a line, and he found himself reaching for her hand again.

He couldn't help touching her. She relaxed her hand in his, and he ran his fingers over hers, holding them. He had to fight the image of what it would've been like to take her to bed and have her under him. He was fidgeting on the stool, feeling suddenly uncomfortable. It had been too long since he'd had a woman under him in bed.

"It is what it is." He couldn't believe he'd said that. It was something his dad always said, and now he was saying the same thing.

"Still, I can't imagine. That's just the ultimate betrayal. Break up, walk away, just don't do that," she said, and something about the way she said it had him really looking at her. "But you didn't answer about the other things you have waiting for you back home. You know, a job, something…" She paused again, and he just looked at her.

A job was something he hadn't figured out. He had an open offer at the feed store as assistant manager, and of course his dad would always have something for him on the ranch, being in the horse business. Jed Friessen was hoping one of his sons would take it on, but Chris just didn't think it was for him.

"Just another job until I figure out my life's passion," Chris said. "Whatever it is, it'll come to me. How about you? Since you already told me there's no special someone in your life, why would Ray tell me you're spoken for?" He hadn't meant to ask, because these questions were just drawing him into a community he was going to be leaving soon anyway. Then he realized how quiet she'd become, how unsettled.

"He shouldn't have said that." She pulled her hand away and tucked both safely in her lap. Anyone could have seen how stiff she was.

"So you're not spoken for," he said again. He'd never heard anyone use that expression. It was as if he'd stepped back in time in this county, with all the weirdness of the day.

She shook her head. "Not spoken for. Ray and I are just friends, in an odd sort of way. He was there for me in a really bad time when I was at my lowest, and I'm sure it's nothing more than him wanting to make sure you didn't mess with me." She glanced away.

"You know what? Now I know there's more," he said. "Like why does he feel he needs to protect you? From what, from who?" He lifted his beer, while JD stared into her white wine. He wondered whether she was going to drink any more of that cheap knockoff, so he reached for the glass and slid it away. "Don't drink that crap. I'll get you a real drink," he said as he lifted his hand to get the attention of the barkeep, a middle-aged man with thinning hair.

"No, no, no, Chris, it's fine, really." She reached over and touched his hand to stop him.

"It's not fine. You can't hide how bad that is, and it'll likely leave you with one of those godawful wine headaches. Come on, what do you really want to drink?" he asked just as the man approached.

"What can I get you?"

He glanced over to JD, who bit her lip, worrying. She glanced to him and then to the barkeep.

"I'll have a whiskey neat, two fingers," she added.

Chris looked over to the sweetness across from him, which reminded him of something wholesome, like apple pie, and he realized there was a lot more to JD than he'd thought. He had just cracked open a layer of this complicated woman.

"Honestly never saw that coming," he said as the barkeep left, and she shrugged.

"What can I say?" she teased in a flirty way.

"How about sharing? Come on, tell me about this deep dark past Ray is trying to protect you from."

He noticed the way she hesitated when the barkeep returned with the glass. She thanked him before he hurried away, then squeezed the glass and took a swallow of the dark liquid. He saw the moment the burn hit her, and she seemed to relish the bite. He could smell it from where he sat, and he realized whatever her past was, it was something she didn't like talking about.

"Once upon a time, there was a young idealistic girl who would've done anything to break out of the predictable. She met a guy, and not just any guy. He was the whole package, handsome, charming, and they were in love.

Then one day they got married, and her father found out." She lifted her glass and downed the rest of the liquor before sliding it away, and she folded her hands in front of her.

"Wow, now that's exactly not what I thought you would say."

She waved to the barkeep across the room and then lifted the empty glass. Evidently, she needed a lot of liquid courage to talk about whatever this was, something that was still smarting. Another glass appeared, and she reached for it before Chris laid his hand over her wrist.

"For what it's worth, I'm sorry," he said. Her gaze flicked over to him and then to his hand, so he pulled back, knowing when a woman didn't want to be touched. When she lifted the glass and took another swallow, he added, "Take it easy on the hard stuff." He wondered where that had come from, since he was known to tie one on when he wanted to. Maybe he was seeing the pain she was trying to drown out.

"You asked," she said as if he were responsible.

"Guilty. So how long were you married?" He didn't know why, but he couldn't help thinking her father had done something, maybe Ray too.

"Not long, and it doesn't matter. What matters is I'm here, and he's not," she said. "So I'm pretty sure there's a jukebox here. How about plugging in some quarters and we dance? Liven up this place."

She lifted the glass and downed the remaining whiskey, and he noted people were staring. The last thing he wanted was to be carrying her out of there and having to explain how he hadn't been responsible for getting her drunk. Then she was off the stool, pulling on his arm.

"Come on," she said. "Dance with me."

He could feel that sweet body pressed against him and knew of the fun they could have, but he didn't know why the locals who were all staring their way bothered him. "You know what?" He stood up and pulled his wallet out, then dumped enough cash on the table to cover the drinks before taking her hand and pulling her toward the door. "Let's get out of here, and you can show me the rest of the finest Martin has to offer."

He wasn't sure what flickered across her expression, but then she pulled her hand from his and was walking toward the door. Chris lifted his hand to the barkeep, gesturing to the money on the table, before he walked out and spotted JD already heading back to the lodge.

"JD, wait," he called out and jogged up to her. He touched her arm, but she ripped it away and went to hit his chest, so he grabbed her arms and held them. "Whoa, whoa, what's going on?" There was something about this moment that made him suspect everything was suddenly going sideways. This could end so badly for him.

Her expression, the misery written across her face, had come out of nowhere. She just gripped his shirt as he slid his hands over her bare arms, letting her stand there.

She looked up and rose, her hands now on his face, and he heard the scrape of his whiskers from two days without shaving. Then she kissed him, soft plump lips that tasted of whiskey and something sweet.

As she pressed closer, his hand slid over the small of her back, and he could feel her respond to him. When she finally pulled back, still fisting her hands in his T-shirt, holding tight, staring up to him, he saw something raw and real in her.

The sexy girl he'd first seen was deeper and more complex than he could have imagined, and in kissing JD, he realized no one had ever tasted sweeter.

Chapter Seven

Had it crossed his mind to lead JD up the stairs to his room, strip her of everything, and ride her like an animal? That was all he'd thought about since she'd laid that kiss on him in the middle of town on the street for everyone to see. Her willingness to feel all his hardness in all her softness wasn't lost on him, which was why it had damn near killed him to lead her toward the door of the lodge where she lived, likely with her parents. He'd kissed her once more, feeling his discomfort, cursing the sweet sway of her ass as she walked away.

She had offered nothing more of an explanation of her once-upon-a-time marriage. There was a story there, and it was enough that it had her wanting to drown it out with a lot of liquor.

Maybe he'd never know, and the evening hadn't answered any of his questions about the overprotective deputy who was so head over heels for her. The man could be a serious problem for him.

He climbed the stairs to his room, fishing the old key on its long plastic keyring from his pocket. When he shoved it in the lock and stepped into the darkened room, a light flicked on, and he damn near crapped his pants as he took in the deputy asshole sitting in a blue easy chair. He instantly searched out his things, seeing his open bag on the double bed. For a second, he had to think about how he'd left it.

He stepped into the room and closed the door, then glanced only once to Ray as he walked over to the bed and searched his bag. Was anything missing? He couldn't tell for sure.

"JD is a real sweet girl," Ray said from where he'd made himself comfortable.

Chris wondered what his options were, exactly. If this were anywhere else and Ray wasn't a cop, he could have called the cops and gotten the guy charged with breaking and entering—except this wasn't an ordinary kind of place, and instead of Chris doing the smart thing and driving back to the main highway and going home, he'd just had to push it with a girl who was beginning to get under his skin in a way he hadn't expected.

"How…" He gestured as he turned. "Why are you even in my room?"

Ray didn't appear to be too interested in answering. "I told you not to hurt her. She's delicate, and she deserves better." He was so matter of fact.

Chris saw again that the man was in love with her, and he wondered just how far he'd go to have her. "I haven't done anything to her. I took her for a drink," he said— though, yes, she'd kissed him, and he'd let her, and he would have taken it further. He still wanted to take it further. He could still taste her on his lips, and just thinking of it had him running his tongue over them again. "So what is this to you? You said she's spoken for, but let me be blunt: There's a big difference between wanting a woman who also wants you and wanting one who doesn't. JD isn't interested in you."

Wasn't it his father who had warned him about pushing it, challenging authority? This was something that came naturally, he figured, considering the trait seemed to run freely in the Friessen family, or rather in the men, as his grandmother had pointed out.

"She doesn't know what she wants." Ray actually pushed himself out of the chair, and it squeaked. "And she doesn't need the likes of you confusing her."

Was this guy serious? Chris was about to laugh but thought better of it. "You cannot tell someone, especially a woman, that she doesn't know her mind. She knows exactly who she is. She may have had some tough breaks and may be hurting, but she isn't interested in you." Chris didn't move. He wasn't going to cower under this asshole.

This time, the deputy let out a harsh laugh, and he wondered now about what JD had said about how harmless Ray and her father were. He didn't see things quite the way she did. Maybe she really didn't know everything they were capable of. "So she told you," Ray said and crossed his arms, and Chris knew enough not to say anything else. "She was only seventeen."

Okay, he hadn't been expecting that, and he wondered whether his face gave it away.

"He was never right for her," Ray continued, "and her father didn't want that kind of life for her. That kind of cowboy drifter."

This was really cryptic now, and Chris thought he should've gotten more out of her. "You can't decide for someone how her life is going to be."

The deputy had a hard look, unforgiving. "That may be right in a lot of circumstances, but the problem is she had no idea who he really was. What her dad did, what I did, was the right thing, and whether she knows it or not, she's better off."

Better off than what? "What did you do to him?" Chris could feel the sweat running down his back. He wondered whether he was giving any sign as to how nervous the deputy made him.

"Gave him a choice: Sign the annulment papers, leave town, and never come back, or JD would learn everything about his three years in state prison. The worst part was that he didn't care about that. What he cared about was not letting JD find out about the fact that for those three years, he had been the plaything for a sexual offender in jail who preferred boys."

Chris just stared at Ray. He didn't know where to start, how to address that, and it took him another second to realize his mouth was gaping. "So he left because he didn't want JD to know he was raped in jail."

Ray took another step toward him, leaning in closer. "Would you?"

Chris couldn't even imagine. It was unthinkable, and even as he opened his mouth, there was nothing he could say. That was the one thing, the one horror, that he was sure he'd take to his grave if it happened to him.

"Yeah, as I thought," Ray said, then started to the door and set his hand on the knob.

"I still don't understand why you would dig into a man's past like that and break up his marriage," Chris said. He didn't know why, but he needed to know, though the fact that he now knew something JD didn't wasn't sitting too well with him.

Ray didn't turn around, but he turned his head to the side, taking in Chris with just a sideways glance. "Because Matt LaCroix would always have been a no-good drifter, and that's someone who isn't good enough to be with JD."

He pulled open the door and turned to face him. "Word of advice, Chris: Move on in the morning."

Then he pulled the door closed, and Chris wondered whether there was more to it, more about this Matt LaCroix and the reason to keep him from JD. He looked in his bag and pulled out the pouch where he kept his extra cash, and he spotted one of his credit cards and healthcare card sticking out. They should have been tucked in along with his passport, which was lying loosely on his shirts.

He pulled out the pouch to see if anything was missing, wondering what it was that Deputy Ray had really been looking for. He had a sick feeling, as he held his ID, that Ray and maybe JD's father were putting his life under a microscope, and he was left to wonder whether the fire he was playing with could very well leave him burned.

Chapter Eight

He brushed back the white lace curtain and took in the sun peeking up past the horizon, then ran a hand over his hair, still damp from the hot shower after a night of restlessness the likes of which he couldn't remember having in a good many years. But then, this was the first time a cop was messing with him, and what made it worse was the unease he couldn't shake, as if some kind of blindside was coming.

Maybe that was why he dialed his cell phone and paced in a circle in his bare feet, wearing just his blue jeans as he took in the rumpled bed. He listened to it ring once, twice, and then worried that he was calling too early.

"This had better be good."

Danny always went right to pissed and irritated when he was woken. He heard a murmur from Evie. Apparently, she'd been asleep too. Chris envied his brother at times for what he had with her. He ran his hand over the back of his neck, pulling at the tension.

"Sorry to wake you. Actually, I have a little problem— or hopefully not, though that might be wishful thinking."

He heard his brother sigh, and he wasn't sure what he said to Evie, but he heard a rustle and then what sounded like the bed squeak before Danny said, "Where are you, exactly, and do Mom and Dad know?"

Of course they didn't know. He'd considered calling his mom to pick her legal brain, but he knew that was about the worst idea ever, because she was a mom first, lawyer second, and she'd likely show up in Martin and face down the sheriff, Deputy Ray, and whoever else dared to mess with her son. A mama bear she was to the bone. His dad would be there too, but mainly to keep his mom from ripping them to shreds. No, he definitely didn't need his mother to rescue him.

"No, I called you first, big brother. I'm in South Dakota, a place called Martin. You know how Mom is. If I start calling with something that isn't just a check-in, she'll freak out." He was looking out the window again, taking in the traffic on the street. The sheriff's car, which had been parked beside his bike, pulled out.

"Are you telling me something has happened that she'll be freaking out about? Are you in trouble? What did you do?" Danny now sounded wide awake.

"Okay, why do you always go there, as if I've done something?" He let out a rough sigh that sounded accusing even to him.

His brother said nothing on the other end.

"Not really trouble, per say," he continued. "It's just something that happened yesterday. I was pulled over by cops, long story. I didn't do anything, and they had no reason to stop me. They had me cuffed and on the ground."

The argument had sounded reasonable in his head, but saying it now, he sounded pathetic. He winced, wondering how to explain what he was feeling.

"And what…?" Danny added rather calmly. "Evidently, there's more, because with you on a bike, there are entire scenarios that go through a cop's mind if he feels he may be threatened. Was anyone hurt? Were you hurt? Start at the beginning and don't leave anything out."

He pulled the phone away from his ear and stared at it. "No, I wasn't hurt," he said. There was still the matter of his cracked visor, which would have to be replaced, but he decided to keep that little bit to himself, considering he didn't like where this was going.

"Then my advice is to let it go."

Hearing his brother say those words had him wanting to yell into the phone, make him understand. Danny was supposed to be on his side, yet he was betraying him. He'd wanted Danny to scream injustice and threaten to sue and ramble on about how his constitutional rights had been trampled all over, but he wasn't.

"How can you say something like that?" Chris said. "They didn't have a right to stop me, treat me like a common criminal and cuff me, and then say it was just a routine traffic stop." He waited, hearing his brother sigh on the other end.

"I'm going to say it again: Let it go. There's always leniency extended to cops. They're on the front line, and if they perceive a threat, it's better that you're cuffed so there's no mistake and you get shot. I understand it may not have been cool, but I've heard many tell me about run-ins with the law, and I want to say to each and every one of them that if they hadn't been doing what they were doing to begin with to attract unwanted attention, which then leads to both sides doing and saying things they shouldn't…" He stopped and sighed again. Chris couldn't remember his brother ever sounding so frustrated.

"Everything okay there, Danny?"

"Sorry, yeah, just school. Interning at a public defender's office means I'm having to see everything bad about a broken system that no one is about to fix. It seems anger only brings out the worst in everyone." He blew out a breath. "Evie and I are going to head up to Mom and Dad's this weekend. I think they expected you back. So, in a roundabout way, did I answer your question?"

He shrugged even though his brother couldn't see him. "Sort of, but that wasn't why I was calling. It was something else. The same cops…well, one of them was in my room last night waiting for me when I got back. He went through my things, my ID, found it and pulled it out of my bag."

There was a lot more he wanted to tell Danny about JD's ex, how they'd forced him to walk away from her. He was still having a lot of trouble getting his head around what he'd heard. It was horrible what had happened to him, something he'd never have wanted the woman he loved to ever find out about him. This was beginning to seem too much like a sick, twisted mess. If he were smart, he'd pack his bag and leave.

There was silence on the other end, and he thought for a second that his brother had hung up. "You still there?" he asked.

"Yeah, still here. Are you telling me you stayed in the same place where you were just complaining about cops overreacting?"

Okay, that was exactly what he hadn't wanted to hear. He'd told himself the same thing as he'd driven into town the day before. "Okay, just hear me out. There's this girl…"

"Are you kidding me?" his brother yelled. "A girl! You don't ever press your luck or get yourself on the wrong side of the law for a girl." Danny actually groaned on the other end. "Do you have any idea how many idiots I see who've managed to get themselves into trouble in the name of love? Girls have men thinking with a part of their anatomy that isn't the brain. And then they're suddenly wondering why their only view is a tiny box with bars."

He pulled in a breath, wondering whether his brother was going to let him get a word in. "Are you finished your rant? It's not what you think."

"Oh, it never is."

When had his brother become so cynical? "Seriously, Danny, it's not like that. She pulled up on the scene yesterday when I was face down on the pavement, cuffed," Chris began, and related the whole story about Ray, his blackmail, and the annulment. "The kind of dirt they found out is something I wouldn't want my girl knowing if it were me."

He imagined his brother telling him to pack his bags and get the hell out of town, but he kept thinking about JD and her sadness and the chemistry that rocked between them. He realized he wasn't ready to go, but at the same time, the forces against him, namely Deputy Ray, would likely do everything to see he left.

"Huh," was all Danny said.

Chris pulled the phone away again and stared at it for a second. "Is that all you're going to say?"

"What do you want me to say, Chris? I know you, and I know you're the last person anyone can tell what to do. You'll dig in, especially when someone tries to make you do something you aren't ready for and don't want to do. But ask yourself, before you get any deeper into something you'd be better off walking away from, is it really about the girl, or is this about getting even with two cops who pushed your buttons? Is the girl just the means to getting your retribution?"

Was Danny kidding? He ran his hand over his hair, stopping at the window again. Another cop car was pulling in, but this time, out climbed Deputy Ray. He could feel his shoulders tense as he stared at the asshole who was determined to be a thorn in his side. He knew the answer.

"I'm not ready to leave just yet. Yes, they got on the wrong side of me, but at the same time, JD is something special. I guess I need to know from you, because of what I learned last night, what kind of information can they dig up on me?" he asked, not that he had anything to worry about.

"Just your credit history, any criminal record, your work history, or any nuisance thing they can find, any complaints filed against you. If they're really smart, with today's technology, they could actually use all that to plant something against you. Or, worse, they could use whatever they find and put quite the spin on it. You're clean, right?"

He couldn't believe Danny had asked that. "Of course I am," he said—except for the parking ticket he'd been handed in Alabama, but he planned on mailing that in.

"Then I wouldn't worry about it. It sounds like these guys are out to make your life miserable, though. My advice, leave, but since I know you, just be careful. You'd better be sure this girl is worth it."

Chris watched as Ray walked up the front steps of the lodge. He thought of JD, her smile, her face. Damn, those eyes. "She is."

"Oh, and just because I'm worried now, you need to tell me exactly where you are. You said in South Dakota?"

Chris rambled off the address as he took in the old window. "Oh, and, Danny, don't mention this conversation to Mom. You know how she is," he added.

"Yeah, yeah, I know, but here's the deal: You call me tonight and every day, same time, until you leave. If you don't call me and check in to reassure me that everything is fine and you're not tossed in a hole someplace, I'll pick up the phone and call both Mom and Dad."

As Chris hung up and pocketed his phone, he wondered at which point in the years to come he'd look back on this and laugh. As he listened to the floor creak and the sounds of the old lodge, he couldn't shake the feeling that had been with him since he'd been pulled over to the side of a deserted highway and been toyed with by two cops

He wondered what the deputy and JD's father, the sheriff, would have in store for him today.

Chapter Nine

"So you didn't tell me how it went last night with that good-looking biker," her mom said as she walked into the kitchen, wearing a peach sundress and matching wedge sandals that clicked as she walked. Her hair was tucked behind her ears and her makeup perfectly applied. Even her nails were painted a light shade of red.

"It was good," JD said. She wiped flour from her hands, unable to shake her worry over what she'd done the night before. She turned away, staring at the oven, and shut her eyes for a second as that knot in her stomach tightened.

She remembered the moment Chris had pulled her out of the bar before she could do anything stupid—like order another whiskey, which would have taken her from light-headed giddiness to sloppy drunk, letting out her inner craziness and allowing everyone in Martin to see what she kept safely tucked away. He'd saved her from a humiliation people wouldn't have let her forget.

Then there was that kiss, that glorious kiss that had rocked her to her toes. She heard the ding of the timer.

"Good, just good?" her mom said, her expression annoyed.

JD turned around and reached for the oven mitts, then opened the old commercial oven and pulled out a tray of lemon ginger scones. The aroma was mouthwatering. She rested the tray on the butcher block counter. "Yup, just good," she said. She tossed her mom an easy smile before Ray walked right into the kitchen, just like he did every morning.

He nodded to her and her mom. He seemed so unsettled, his icy blue eyes landing on her, so different from the vivid blue of Chris's. Ray seemed so much a part of this place, but he gave all his attention to her, showing up at the same time every morning. She wondered now when it was that he'd started checking in on her.

"Wow, something smells good," he said, leaning against the sink. He smiled over to her, but there was something different in that smile today.

"Scones, help yourself. It'll be just a continental breakfast this morning. There're blueberry muffins too, and bread and jam are already set up in the dining room. Oh, and coffee should be ready out there…"

"Hello?"

JD heard Chris's deep voice and didn't miss the way Ray stood straighter and dragged his gaze over to the swinging kitchen door behind him. JD tossed the oven mitts beside the tray of scones on the island, and her feet started moving before Ray could take a step to the door. She pushed it open to find him in the empty dining room, wearing a red shirt and blue jeans, tall, handsome, sexy.

She was in trouble. What was it about that red hair, that tall and rugged look, that magic in his deep blue eyes? Her heart thudded, and as she kept walking right toward him, the smile that touched his lips had her resting her hand awkwardly over her chest.

"Good morning," she said. Her hand went to her hair, which she'd pulled back into a messy bun, and for a moment she worried about how she looked. It was pure instinct to smooth her hand over the white apron she wore over her blue and white striped sundress. Her feet were bare, shoved in the flip flops she seemed to live in come summer.

"I started down the steps and was hit by the aroma of fresh baking coming from that kitchen," Chris said. "It has my mouth watering." He looked past her at the empty tables.

JD gestured to the coffee pot, which seemed to have just finished brewing, wanting to kick herself all because Chris Friessen was still there, smiling at her in a way that made her wonder when the rug would be yanked out from under her.

"There's coffee," she said. "Help yourself. Breakfast is just baked goods this morning. I was about to bring out the tray of muffins and scones. The bread is over there, beside the toaster. Just toast your own. Jam, butter, everything is here." She gestured to the side table she always set up for breakfast, ready for anyone staying there and those who stopped in, like Ray.

Chris was staring past her, the smile gone, and she realized that the air was suddenly weighted with a tension that filled her with such unease. JD turned, her eyes going right to where he was looking. Her mom and Ray were standing in the doorway, watching them. Their expressions were intrusive, and they didn't even try to hide it.

"Why don't you join me for breakfast?" Chris said. "Kind of wanted to have a minute alone to talk with you."

She glanced back to Chris and then to Ray and her mom, who were still standing there. It was ridiculous.

"Mom, can you put the scones on the big oval tray on the island along with the rest of the baked goods and bring it on out here? Ray, just help yourself to whatever's in there. You know where it is." She gestured to him before turning back to Chris. "You know what? I think I will. Let me grab a coffee. Not hungry, though. Had a yogurt earlier. If I ate what I baked every day, I'd be close to three hundred pounds." She waited only a second, unable to explain her relief when her mom and Ray walked back into the kitchen.

Chris was right beside her at the window, the light spilling in, as she grabbed two mugs, turned them over, and poured coffee in one and then the other.

"I forgot milk," she said. "Do you…?"

"Black, don't worry about it," he said. He took one just as her mom walked back out of the kitchen with a tray filled with muffins and scones and set it on the breakfast table alongside the plates, napkins, and utensils.

"Well, Chris, so how did you sleep?" her mom said, lingering a little too close to him. "Good, I hope. We really do take pride in our little place and want everyone who stays here to feel as if they're at home." She gave a bright flirty smile that reminded JD of why she'd been in a beauty pageant. It was the smile she tossed to every handsome red-blooded man.

"Thanks, ma'am, I did," he said.

JD noted his manners as her mom waved her hand and touched his arm, another thing she often did. She was a touchy-feely kind of person, especially in social situations, where she took over a room, or when a good-looking man was speaking with her. Maybe that was why she could feel her nerves again.

"Thanks, Mom. We got it from here," JD said, cutting in before her mom could say anything else. Ray was standing there in the dining room again, just watching so quietly.

"Okay, point taken, JD," her mom said. "If you need anything, you just holler. I'll be in the kitchen with Ray. Come on, Ray." Her mom actually swept her hand and pushed open the kitchen door, and Ray lingered a second before tossing another odd look to Chris, the kind of look that again ramped up the tension in the room.

She knew he wasn't happy, and for the first time, she realized she had to acknowledge what he was feeling for her. Even though he hadn't said anything to her, she wasn't a fool. From all the hints and the rumors, she realized that her family and the people of Martin had assumed there was something between them. She needed to shut that door and figure out what she really wanted.

Chris was still staring at the swinging kitchen door. His fun, flirty smile was long gone, and what was left was a man who wasn't going to be messed with.

Maybe that was why she touched his forearm, feeling the strength radiating from it. He pulled his gaze back to her and then to the baked goods as if remembering they were there. He loaded up a plate. "Let's grab a seat over by the window, over there. It's likely the most privacy we'll have."

She started over to the table, and Chris followed with a heaping plate of muffins, scones, and butter. She reached for a napkin and knife for him and rested them on the table as she sat down, scooting the wooden chair in, and she watched as he towered over her and then settled the plate down in the center of the table as he took the seat across from her. The wooden chair creaked.

"Listen, I wanted to talk to you about last night," he

said before taking a bite of a scone. He groaned, a sound that never got old. There was fun, flirty Chris again.

She smiled as she lifted her mug and took a sip of coffee.

"Oh, man, I thought last night's dinner was fantastic, but these are a work of art." He held the scone up as if to show her, then shoved the rest in his mouth and chewed before resting both his elbows on the table. Looking right and then left, he wiped his hands. "You know, you shared some pretty heavy shit last night. As soon as that door was opened, I could see you have a gaping wound from a heap of stuff you haven't figured out. Then there was that kiss," he said, looking right at her.

He waited a moment before picking up a warm blueberry muffin and breaking it open so the berries gushed out. He took a bite, his gaze going from the muffin to her, and her heartbeat kicked up again.

What the hell could she say to explain what had happened? She wished she could go back and close her damn mouth. She'd never spoken about Matt with anyone but Ray. What was it about Chris that had her wanting to spill everything? At what point would it be too much? She didn't know how to feel.

She shrugged, gripping the mug, seeing the white of her knuckles. "I wanted to kiss you. Was it terrible?" She flicked her gaze back over to him, unsure of what she'd see looking back at her, remembering every detail of that kiss, touching him, his lips, the way he'd gently run his hand over her.

He said nothing for a second, then shook his head as he chewed and swallowed. "No, but I wonder if the reason for the kiss was that you needed a distraction. Not that I mind, although you don't seem the type to do the quick and dirty."

She nearly choked on her coffee, not expecting that kind of bluntness. He didn't seem shy about it. Did he have any idea, she wondered, that she'd likely have gone willingly to his bed the night before and screwed his brains out? But this morning, she would have…what, regretted it? Just looking at him now, she was considering again how wrong it was supposed to be.

She took in the heavy gaze, those distinct blue eyes. This man didn't have a shy bone in his body. Maybe that was why she wanted him the way she did. She had to remind herself where she was, so she lifted her mug to take a swallow of coffee and try to pull it together. It wasn't right to want a man like Chris as much as she did.

"Are you looking for me to say out loud that kissing you was the best thing ever and I want to do it again? If you'd taken me up the stairs to your room last night, would I have slept with you, had sex with you…?" She stopped talking when he stilled. She should have been shocked, saying those words to him. She'd never said that to anyone.

She didn't know why she was suddenly completely willing to put herself out there with Chris. Maybe it was because he didn't look away, as if trying to figure out a way to peel back everything she hid from everyone. She dropped her gaze to her mug again. It was easier to look at without feeling so exposed.

"I talked about something last night that I don't talk about. Yeah, it still hurts that Matt ran off, that he left, that he caved under whatever pressure my dad leveled on him, but I realize now that what hurts more is the fact that he didn't love me enough to stay and fight for me." She touched her chest.

He wasn't looking away. His gaze lingered on her chest, her face, her eyes, all of her.

"I don't really want to talk about him," she continued

with a dry voice that didn't sound like her own. "That heavy shit, as you said, has everything to do with a man who ran after saying I was his everything. That kind of lie made me feel unworthy, unloved, unwanted, and hollow."

She tried to picture Matt, his light hair, his lean features, his smile—but the image no longer gutted her as she stared across the table to Chris. He seemed different, but he was just a man. He would likely be on his way that day, and she'd never see him again. Maybe that was why it seemed so easy to share the pain she never shared with anyone.

He took a breath as he leaned back, resting his arm over the other chair. She felt the distance he was trying to instigate, pulling away from her. She expected him to slide back his chair and say…what, goodbye? But all he did was narrow his gaze as he looked out the old window beside them, which was in much need of some paint and maintenance.

Evidently, she'd said too much. She fought the urge to talk in the lingering uncomfortable silence. Maybe being touchy-feely had been exactly the wrong approach. But what was the right one with a guy like Chris?

"Do you know what your father did to make him leave, make him sign the papers and walk away?" he said. It took her a minute to understand, and he was still looking out the window as he said it. She could feel the frown and the pull of her brows.

That was the million-dollar question, the one she'd screamed at her father. She'd even asked Ray, but all she'd ever been told was that Matt had shown his true colors, whatever that was supposed to mean.

"Does it matter?" she replied, unable to keep the sadness from her voice.

It had been four years since her father walked through

the door of the kitchen that day. She'd been trying a new recipe, Matt's favorite, chicken and dumplings, a dish she'd never made again. That moment would forever be burned into her memory. The day had been hot, and she'd worn her pink dress, Matt's simple ring on her finger. Her father had said nothing as he placed the papers in front of her, and she had stared in horror at the bold lettering, *Annulment*, with Matt's signature at the bottom. She'd never seen or heard from Matt again. She'd burned the dress and flushed the ring.

But the ache in her heart seemed different now, here with Chris.

"It could matter," he said, leveling those brilliant blue eyes on her. There was something in his expression that she couldn't read. "Some things happen that a man would never want a woman to know about."

Unease suddenly settled between them, and she went to lift her mug but settled it back on the table with a clatter, feeling an anger she hadn't in a long time.

"No, Chris. The only thing that matters is that when he said he loved me more than anything, what he really meant was that he didn't love me enough to fight for me. That says everything about a man. So whatever this is, please don't." She gestured toward him and then fisted her hand beside her mug, feeling her anger over something that had happened so long ago.

Chris tapped the table, but the tension still lingered. "You want to get out of here?"

For a moment, she wasn't sure what he was getting at, what he was trying to accomplish. But he was still there, and the way he was looking at her confused the hell out of her. She should say no, but she found herself wanting to do something different that would break her out of this monotony. She also knew that she wasn't ready to say goodbye to Chris.

"I do," she said. She stood up, untied her apron, and tossed it over the back of the chair, then smoothed down the front of her dress.

There was Chris now in front of her, standing so tall, in her space. He slid his fingers under her chin, a touch she hadn't expected. She realized she could look at this man forever and never tire of it.

"Let's go for a ride," he said.

He reached for her hand and pulled her along behind him to the front door, and as he opened it, his hand slid down and around her back, pulling her closer to him. Without liquid courage, JD went up on her toes and pressed a kiss to those full soft lips. She tasted him and sighed, thinking she could kiss him forever.

S he was perched behind him on the back of his bike, wearing the spare helmet he always had tucked in the bottom of the compartment. It was just a simple, dorky thing, without full face gear, but she didn't seem to mind. She leaned against him, her hands around him, all her gorgeous softness pressed into him.

She tapped his shoulder and gestured to a sign for a river up ahead, and he turned, going down the unpaved back-country road, gravel and dirt, just riding. Something about being on a bike and traveling beat a car any day, and having JD pressed against him made this moment pure heaven.

About six miles in, he parked at a spot by a trail that opened up to the fast-moving river. There were trees and tall grass, and there was no one around, from what he could see. He turned off his bike and then tapped the kick-stand down as he pulled off his helmet, turning to JD, who was still leaning against him with that beautiful smile that lit up her face.

"This is a great fishing spot on the weekends, and a great spot to come and think," she said.

It was automatic, his arm going back, his hand touching her leg as she stepped down and tried as gracefully as she could to get off the bike in a dress. Fortunately, he caught a hint of her thigh as she slipped off. He didn't even try to hide his appreciation as he stepped down and helped her unfasten her helmet after resting his on the seat.

He took in the mess of her hair falling from a clip in the back as he lifted her helmet off, and she reached up and let it fall free, tossing back her head. He took in her long, slender neck. Of course, he imagined his lips there, tasting her, and running his hands over her glorious body. There was just something about JD. He didn't want this moment to end.

She was looking at him, heat in her eyes, and he knew she wanted him as much as he did her. Then she stepped around him, sliding her hand around his waist. The teasing spark was there again.

"Hey, wait a second," he said, pulling her to a stop, his hand linking with hers, feeling the softness she seemed to exude as she stepped closer. He'd never met anyone like her and likely never would again.

"Come on, I want to show you a perfect spot—well, one I like to come to every now and then, where I look out at the water and just think, with no one around. I've never shared this with anyone, but you'll see what I mean..." The way she said it made him feel something he hadn't with anyone before.

She was leading him up a trail, past a crop of trees to a bank that sloped gently to the water. It was shady, and he could see the beauty here, hearing the water lap against the bank, the sound of the gentle breeze, breathing in the magic of this place. Just sitting and watching the river go by, they were so sheltered that he could've sworn they were in their own little world.

She sat on the ground, her knees up and her arms around her legs, even though her cotton dress rode up to show off more of her creamy thigh. He realized she didn't care. Then she patted the ground beside her, and he couldn't resist. There was an ease about her now that hadn't been there before at the lodge. He sat beside her in the dry August grass.

"You're right, this is perfect," he said, leaning back on his elbows, watching her back.

She was close to him, touching him, and she angled her head. The warmth in those brown eyes flickered, the color of honey. Meeting someone new always came with that beginning chemistry that zinged off the charts, but with JD it was something different, something more, something deeper. This had never happened with a woman before. He had to remind himself to breathe before he did something he shouldn't.

"I would come out here and sit for hours alone," she said. "It was wonderful to just take in the water, listening to it ripple and flow. I could be alone for a while and just think about life without having to worry about pretending everything was okay."

By the way she was talking, he wondered whether she was thinking of Matt again. If only she knew the truth, would he be driving her right back to him?

"Mind if I ask why your father and Ray did what they did? Why drive Matt away?" he asked. *And why the roadside show when they pulled me over with such rough dramatics?* He didn't ask that last part even though he wanted her to explain the heavy hand at the forefront of the town.

She shrugged. "Over-protective, over-worrying, and micromanaging my life. I wondered if it was about who

Matt was, just a hired hand on a ranch outside town, running cattle and doing everything that went with that. My dad always said that kind of person would never be anything or have anything, but I wouldn't listen. When Matt and I stood before the justice of the peace and got married, he insisted we just call my parents to tell them, and we could see them another day, but I said no, because they were my parents and the phone was too impersonal.

"I made Matt drive us back to the lodge to share what I believed was such happy news, only to find my dad and my mom sitting with the very judge who'd just married us. A second passed before my dad yelled like I'd never heard him before, not at me. I realized Matt had likely understood something I hadn't. My father ordered my mom to take me to my room, and, long story short, that was the last time I ever laid eyes on Matt. I disappointed my father that day, and he's never let me forget it." JD had been staring out over the water with sadness.

"And Ray, where does he fall into all this?" Chris was starting to think her father might only be okay with his daughter being with Ray, that he'd already picked a husband for JD, and she hadn't fallen in line with what he'd expected.

She slid around to lie on her stomach, propped up on her elbows, so close to Chris that he could feel her heat as she glanced at him with those amazing eyes, which didn't seem to hide anything from him in that moment. If he just leaned over a bit more, her lips would be right there, and he could kiss her. He wanted to.

"Ray has worked for my Dad for years. They've been friends longer. How does he fit? He's always been there, as if he's slipped into our family. I don't know what makes Ray different from Matt in my family's eyes. All I know is I'm not interested in him romantically. He's a friend, that's all, and that's all he'll ever be, nothing more. There can't be, because the only man I have feelings for is the guy who's here with me now."

She slid up on her knees so slowly and leaned over to him, pressing her lips to his. It was so soft and gentle. He allowed his hand to run over the back of her head, holding her close as he tasted her. She angled her head, pressing her hands over his cheeks before pulling back just a bit. The energy had ratcheted up, and he was dying to run his hands over her, to touch her, to feel her, to taste every inch of her.

She pulled back, her hands still on his face. Her breath was warm, and he watched her hesitation as she pulled in her lower lip as if the taste of him was everything. His hand slid over her cheek and through her hair, pulling her back to him. He wasn't done, not by a longshot, and then he had her on the ground, under him.

Her touch was like nothing before, like no one before. How was it that a stranger could suddenly be everything? This was crazy, and maybe that was why he leaned in and pressed his lips to hers, taking what she was offering. He deepened the kiss and was on his side on the ground, holding her, pulling her to him. His hand traced over her bottom and to the hem of her dress, and she slid her leg over his, her hands running over his chest.

He lifted the light soft cotton, feeling the lacy edge of her underwear, her perfectly rounded ass, her thighs, all that soft skin. Her lips were pressed to his, and he was pulled into this moment of just her and him, feeling the way she tugged at his T-shirt as she pressed her body closer with just clothes between them.

Dammit, he wanted to free himself and have her naked under him, feeling her skin to skin. He didn't want to go slow. Her hand slid under his shirt, tracing up his back, over his spine, and down over his jeans, his ass, pulling him closer. It was pure instinct to pull back and slide his fingers under her dress, lift it over her head, and allow it to fall to the ground. He took in her bikini underwear, white with lace trim, and her bra, which the most gorgeous, round, plump breasts he'd ever seen were spilling out of.

She was breathing deeply as he reached around and unhooked her bra, allowing the straps to slide down her arms. She pulled it off, and he took it from her and tossed it over to where her dress was. She went up onto her knees as he sat up and slipped his fingers in her underwear to edge them down. She maneuvered to the side so he could slip them off, and there she was with nothing at all on.

He reached out to touch one glorious breast, feeling the weight and then running his hand down the flat of her stomach and lower as she lay back down, her arms lifted above her head. She was gorgeous, the most beautiful woman he'd ever seen, and the sound that drifted past her lips was killing him, having him wanting to bury himself in her right then. She was gorgeous and responsive, and he needed to feel her around him. He yanked off his shirt and stood up to take off his pants.

Then he heard something.

"Freeze! Just what the hell is going on here?"

He couldn't believe who was there. JD screamed and grabbed her dress, pressing it over her breasts, and Chris jerked his head around to see Ray, the asshole deputy, staring at JD as she did her best to cover her nakedness. It was pure instinct for Chris to step over to JD to hide her from Ray and give her the only privacy he could. The look the deputy gave him was nothing short of murderous, and he didn't think he'd ever get the image from his mind. From the way her cheeks flushed, he was positive JD was absolutely mortified.

"This is private," he snapped, glancing back to her. He grabbed his shirt and held it up so she could get dressed. "You okay?" he said, though she wouldn't look up at him.

"Turn around," Ray ordered.

Chris knew Ray had his hand on his gun, and he was way past being reasoned with, considering Chris had been two seconds away from getting lucky with the girl he wanted. Guys just didn't handle that kind of thing that well. He could see the cop was considering ways to make sure Chris disappeared forever.

"Give me a minute, would you?" Chris said. "For the love of God, man, turn around so JD can put her clothes on. You're embarrassing her."

A shade of pink hit the deputy's cheeks, as if those words were enough for him to realize what an asshole he was being. He turned his head but didn't move. "Just until she gets dressed," he said, and Chris didn't miss the warning.

JD was fastening her bra, and he reached for her dress and handed it to her. As she pulled it over her head, a blush rose again over her cheeks, and her eyes were filled with the same fury he was feeling. Of course, she was embarrassed. Chris was sure once he got past his blinding rage, he'd realize it was the humiliation that was driving it, considering this deputy was pushing him in ways no one ever had before. He was having to remind himself why it wasn't okay to fight back—namely because of the badge pinned to his chest, the gun he was waiting to reach for, and the fact that the man could make sure he never saw the light of day again.

Chris reached out and helped JD up, holding her hand. He could feel her tremble, taking in the emotion in her face. He didn't let go as he touched her chin with his other hand, running his thumb over her cheek, allowing his touch to reassure her. "Sorry," he mouthed, then tried to give her an easy smile, one he knew didn't reach his eyes.

She said nothing, but he could feel how tense she was, so he pulled on his shirt, still feeling his discomfort. His jeans were snug, and of course she could see, and so could the deputy. He couldn't remember anyone ever making him feel this small before.

"So what did you do, follow us?" he said. He knew he sounded accusing, turning and making a point to keep JD behind him. He even reached back, touching her to keep her there. She had to know, as he felt her hand slide over his arm, touching him, holding on to him, stepping closer to him. He glanced down to the spot where he'd been lying moments earlier with a woman he'd never expected to want this much.

"You take off with the sheriff's daughter on the back of a bike and don't think there are repercussions?" Ray said. "And this, finding you here like this, with her, naked in a public place…" He pulled his cuffs from his pouch and dangled them, and all Chris could do was stare in horror. "Turn around and lock your hands behind your head."

For a second, Chris didn't think the man was serious, but evidently he was, as he took a step closer, the cuffs dangling and his hand still touching his gun. Yeah, the anger simmering in those steel-blue eyes let Chris know Ray meant every word. He wondered if the man was willing him to do something so he could shoot him.

"Look, this is ridiculous," Chris said. "You followed us and were watching, and now you want to arrest me for—"

"I said turn around, now."

"Ray, stop this!" JD snapped. He could hear her fury. "This is beyond embarrassing and not okay." She stepped out from behind him, though he tried to stop her. He could see the mix of emotions, from anger to humiliation, that filled her eyes, her expression, as she stared over to a man so in love with her that Chris feared he'd likely be on the receiving end of the brunt of his anger. He didn't have a clue how to defuse this and make Ray realize he'd crossed so many lines.

"JD, this doesn't concern you," Ray said. "Now, do I have to tell you one more time to turn around and put your hands behind your head?"

Chris knew he was out of options, out of ways to reason with a man who wasn't about to be reasoned with. He took in the gun and turned around, linking his hands behind his head. The steel cuffs were slapped on, and JD stared in horror as his arms were wrenched back. He grunted at the sharp pain that shot through his shoulders and wrists as the cuffs tightened to the point of being painful.

"What the hell, Ray? You can't do this," she said. "This is crazy. On what grounds are you arresting Chris?" She was furious, pulling on his arm.

He knew she was about to shove Ray or something, so he moved in front of her, taking a step on pure instinct in an impossible situation. "JD, no!"

Ray grabbed his arm. "Stay out of this," he said. He was gripping just above his elbow in a spot he had to know would hurt.

Every emotion Chris was feeling was written all over JD: the anger, the outrage, the embarrassment. Chris stumbled a bit as he was pulled back and shoved.

"Get going now," Ray said. "JD, you too. I'll drop you back at home."

Chris started walking down the trail, and JD fell in beside him as Ray grabbed his arm to keep him moving. "So how about filling me in on the deal here, the reason

I'm cuffed again? Or am I actually under arrest this time?" he said.

He waited for the deputy to say something. From the way he was gripping his arm, walking so close to him, he could feel his anger and knew well every step he had missed in the arrest. He hadn't been mirandized, and he didn't have a clue what he was being charged with.

"Indecent exposure—and being an asshole," the deputy said.

Chris had to fight the urge to laugh. He'd been fully clothed, with just his shirt off, which was no crime for a man. It seemed Ray was still figuring out the charges, and that should have worried him. He glanced down at JD, who was right beside him, her lips pressed tight, shaking her head. She was as aware as he was that she'd been the one completely naked, lying on the ground by the river.

"I see," he said. And he did. This cop was willing to do anything to see to it that he stayed away from JD.

Chapter Eleven

JD pulled her arms over her stomach, staring in horror as Chris was put where criminals were stuck, in the back of Ray's caged and locked police car. Ray still hadn't looked at her, and what made this moment worse than anything was that he had made her feel, for the first time, as if she were dirty.

He gestured to the passenger side and escorted her around, then pulled open the door and waited for her to slide in. She stared out the window, seeing Chris's bike was being left there as if it were abandoned. Ray backed up with a lot of gas and spun around in a way that had her gripping her seat belt as he drove back out toward the highway.

She couldn't believe he had followed them. It was beyond anything she could even have imagined, and she was still embarrassed that he'd seen her naked. But Chris was the one getting the brunt of everything.

"You can't do this, Ray," she said. "It's wrong on so many levels. Chris did nothing wrong. You want to arrest and charge someone with something, then you charge me.

I was the one without clothes on—but let me point out to you the number of people who've gone skinny dipping out this way and had sex at the riverside. Are you telling me you've arrested all of them and charged them with… with…?" She was so mad she was having a hard time talking.

Chris was just sitting there in back. From what she could see through the black wire mesh, his expression gave nothing away, and she didn't have a clue what he was thinking.

"You were doing more than skinny dipping," Ray said. "JD, what the hell were you thinking, going off with him? Do you have any idea what could have happened? You don't know anything about him!" He gave it a lot of gas as he turned onto the highway, the tires squealing.

They were only a few miles from town and would be there in no time. She figured a talk with her dad would likely clear this up, but then what? Chris would be gone. Absolutely, this time he would be. He was smart and would look after his own health, and, knowing the kind of trouble that would be coming on him because of her, he would see she wasn't worth it. It had happened before.

"I know enough, Ray, and I also know you've gone too far. Sneaking up on us like that… We weren't bothering no one. That was a private moment between me and Chris."

The look he gave her before turning back to the road was that of a man who had his mind made up. He wasn't hearing her. She'd always been able to talk to Ray, to reason with him, but she felt now that he wasn't about to be reasoned with where Chris was concerned.

She let out a breath and looked back to him. "I'm sorry," was all she could get out. She still didn't have a clue what he was thinking.

When Ray pulled in and parked in front of the jail, he

turned off the car and stepped out without a word to JD before pulling open the back door of the cruiser. "Out," was all he said to Chris.

JD climbed out and gave the door a shove closed, then followed behind. Chris's wrists were still cuffed, and Ray was pulling on his arm, shoving him inside the double doors with their clouded Plexiglas, over to the front counter, behind which sat Edna Hayes, the clerk. She was JD's mom's age but three dress sizes larger, and her expression said everything as she took in JD, then Chris, who was being led to the back, where the cells were.

JD couldn't see any more but heard the metal clang of the bars and the lock clicking as she stood where she was, resting her hand on the stained, aged dark wood of the counter.

"Do I want to know what this is about?" Edna asked.

Just then, JD's father stepped out from his office. He stared at her and then back to where Ray had gone, waiting for someone to fill him in. His smile faded as soon as he saw her face. She had never been able to hide how she was feeling.

"Daddy, you need to talk some sense into Ray," she said. "After what he did today, he's gone too far. He crossed too many lines."

She could hear footsteps, and Ray appeared from around the corner. "That biker kid is locked up in back," he said, then gestured with his thumb. Something passed between him and her father, and she realized there was so much more at play here.

The sheriff said nothing to JD as Ray strode across the room, toward his office, right past her. He stopped in front of her dad, and whatever he said, the private discussion was setting her on edge. All she knew was that in the next second, Ray was walking over to her, and he stopped in front of her.

"Ray, you take her home now," her father said in a tone she'd not heard in years.

Ray put his hand on her shoulder as if he had every right to lead her, to move her, but she pushed it away and stepped back.

"No, enough, both of you," she snapped. "This is crazy! You want to arrest someone, you arrest me. I was the one who was naked, not Chris. Yes, I was there, ready and willing to have sex with him out by that river—which I guarantee half the town did in their younger years."

She took in Edna's gaping mouth and knew the gossip would likely have spread over half the town by nightfall. JD lifted her wrists in the air with a dramatic flair for Ray to cuff her, daring him to do something. She could see the moment he was about to reach out to try to move her along, so she stepped back again.

"There's no way you can charge Chris with indecent exposure," she said. "Not even your judge friend can make that happen, especially when I go in there and stand up and tell my side of it, making sure it's me you arrest, me you charge. If you insist on this ridiculous charge, I'll get so loud and tell everyone who'll listen that it was me, not Chris. I'll be such a pain in the ass—"

"Enough!" her father yelled.

Her heart was hammering, and by his expression, the anger that simmered in his face, she knew she'd accomplished what she needed to. He gestured sharply, pissed off, not saying a word more, and she waited, wondering what would happen next. He glanced to her, his hands on his duty belt, and in his expression were both disbelief and disappointment.

Then Ray walked back toward where he had locked up

Chris. In the minute that she waited with Edna, staring from her to her father, she heard the lock click and the squeak of the metal bars, and she tried to figure out when her father and Ray had taken over the running of her life. She didn't remember it happening. She didn't remember when she'd allowed herself to slide into the passenger seat and let others run her life for her. Or maybe that was all they'd ever done, and this was the first time she was seeing what was really happening.

Chris appeared, walking ahead of Ray, and his expression was that of a man who'd been pushed too far. His gaze sought her out. As he walked around the desk, she thought he might just keep on walking right past her, right on out of there. Instead, he stopped in front of her and slid his hand under her chin, his large warm hand. She realized in that second how much she'd wanted him. She gripped his wrist. Something about touching him now and seeing he was okay should have calmed her.

"You okay?" he said, though she should've been asking him that very thing.

"Yeah, you? I'm so sorry."

He only nodded as he slid his hand over her cheek and down to her shoulder, then took her hand and guided her away from the desk, from her father and Ray, outside.

"I'm so sorry, Chris. I can't believe…" *That Ray followed us, and my father encouraged it.*

"Well, let's not linger around here. I need to get my bike." He was still holding her hand, and she walked down the steps with him, feeling the day beginning to warm.

"Let's go back to the lodge," she said. "I'll get my car and drive you back there." It was only a few blocks, and then what? She needed to know but feared asking. He'd likely get on his bike and ride out of town, and she'd never see him again. Maybe that was why the ache grew in her chest.

"I heard you in there," he said. "You know, you can really carry on if you want to. Can't believe you said what you did to your father, to Ray."

As they walked, she rested her other hand on his arm. "Seriously, Chris, that was a complete abuse of authority—and I would have told the judge so, you know. I'd have called anyone and everyone who would listen if they hadn't let you go."

She hadn't expected Chris to laugh. He let go of her hand and pulled her closer, his arm around her shoulder as they walked. She slid hers around his back and leaned into him.

"You think that was what happened with Matt?" she said. They walked slower, just the two of them, hearing the cars but not seeing the faces behind the wheels.

He was shaking his head as they crossed the street. "If you knew the real reason why he left, would you go looking for him?"

Something about the way Chris kept bringing him up had her looking at his face as they walked, his arm still around her. He had tensed, and that bothered her.

"That ship has long since sailed," she said. "Maybe, at one time, I needed to know. But it doesn't matter anymore. He left. End of story."

Ahead was the lodge, its steps leading up, and they stopped walking. His hand fell away, and he stepped in front of her. She didn't know why, but she lifted her hand and pressed it over his chest, feeling the breath he pulled in.

"You know, Chris, you keep bringing him up. I wonder if I shouldn't have mentioned him, but I did. If I was still pining for him or wanted all those answers, though, I wouldn't be standing here with you."

For a second, she worried she'd said too much, but Chris slid his hand over hers and held it. He led her up the stairs to the lodge and opened the door, and all she could hear as she stepped in was the ticking of the old clock and the beat of her heart.

"I'll get my keys," she said, pulling her hand away, but Chris reached for it again.

"No, not yet," he said. He pulled her with him as he started up the steps, taking one and then another, holding her hand, and she followed, knowing exactly why.

For the first time she could remember since Matt, JD truly believed she was doing something just for herself.

Chapter Twelve

Chris closed the door to his room and took in the rumpled bed, yesterday's clothes tossed over the chair where the deputy had been sitting just the night before. Then he took in JD, who was gorgeous and wide eyed and there with him.

He was furious with Ray and her father, who were doing their best to make everything miserable for him. Something about someone toying with him just made him dig his feet in more. It was that stubbornness his dad had warned him about, saying it could have him going one step too far, ending up in the kind of trouble he wouldn't be able to take back.

But as he took a step over to JD, he wasn't thinking of walking away. He couldn't.

He stood in front of her and leaned down and kissed her, her arms going around his neck as he lifted her and ran his hands over her ass, feeling the rounded perfection. He drowned in her, tasting her, feeling all her softness pressed into him. He heard her sandals hit the floor as he had her on the bed, and she was on her knees. He lifted her dress and tossed it over her head.

"I think we've been here once before," he said, "and I'm eager to get back to where we were before we were interrupted."

She reached back and unfastened her bra as he pulled off his T-shirt and tossed it to the floor. There were just too many clothes between them, but now they had a closed and locked door. She was sitting back on the bed, pulling off her underwear, and Chris kicked off his shoes and socks, unzipped his jeans, and stepped out of them. He was on the bed, over top of her, and her arms were around him, pulling him down, pulling him closer into all that softness.

He was kissing her again, then pulled away. "I swear I've never tasted anything sweeter," he said. He kissed her neck and lower, running his hand over her breast and tracing the soft perfection of her skin. He could take it slow, make this last.

She pressed her head back into the mattress and breathed out, "Chris…I want you inside me."

He lowered his head, teasing her as he pressed a kiss to her stomach, but waiting and teasing could come later. "Shit, condom. Uh, give me a second," he said, then went up on his knees and stepped off the bed. The agony was killing him, how ready he was.

He reached into his bag on the floor and touched the foil packages in the side pocket. He never left home without condoms. He made quick work of covering himself, and then he was back on the bed, his hands on her thighs, spreading them wide as she lay there with her arms over her head, waiting for him and watching every move he made. He didn't pull his gaze as he slid inside her, and for a second, he was positive he'd died and gone to heaven.

"Chris, please move," she pleaded, wrapping her legs around his.

He leaned down and pressed a kiss to her lips, his forehead against hers, and moved inside her slowly, out and then in again. She whimpered, and he kissed her, her hands touching him, pulling him closer. In that moment, they were just her and him, a guy and a girl who had just met. There was so much more to her than he had realized. JD had somehow snagged a corner of his heart.

He moved again, pressed another kiss to her, and said, "Hang on." He knew he couldn't hold back. As he started to move faster, longer, harder, rocking her, he vaguely heard her cry out, lost in the moment of just her and him and a passion that was beyond anything, feeling everything around him explode.

HE DIDN'T KNOW what had awoken him. He opened his eyes and took in JD, sound asleep in his arms. Her long silky hair spilled over the pillow, and her head was on his shoulder, her legs entwined with his. Then he heard it again, a tapping on the door.

He managed to slip out of bed, and she stirred a moment but didn't wake up. Chris took a second to just look at that gorgeous body, recalling the best sex he'd ever had. Something about how she lay there asleep, so vulnerable, had him reaching down and pulling up the sheet to cover her.

He walked around the bed, reached for his jeans, still in a heap on the floor, and pulled them on. Then he opened the door a crack to see her mother in the hallway. Alice Cayhill had the same honey-blond hair and the same eyes. He didn't know why, but he didn't want to wake JD, so he stepped outside and pulled the door closed behind him, running his hand over his naked chest.

Her mother didn't try to hide her approval of his body. He knew he looked good, and apparently she wasn't shy, as she made a face and nodded. There was just something about this woman that he hadn't been able to figure out.

"So I heard what happened," she said. "Half the town is talking about you and my daughter. Just thought I'd let you know I had someone pick up your bike, and it's back out front." She linked her fingers together and tossed him an easy smile.

He took in the dimly lit hallway and didn't know what to say. Which side of the fence was Alice sitting on? Was she for her husband and Ray or for her daughter?

"Thank you," he said, then didn't add any more, because he could hear his mom in his head, and Danny too, that lawyer stuff: *You've said all you need to. Now shut up.* He rolled his shoulders, wondering what was coming around the corner and whether he'd be ready for it.

"You care for my daughter?" Alice asked.

He didn't know what to say to that and knew he made a face. "Of course I do. She's…special."

"But you'll get on your bike and ride out of town and likely never see her again."

The way she said it, it sounded as if she'd made up her mind about him already. She was no longer smiling that flirty smile. No, he could see he should never dismiss her as a potential problem for him.

He pulled in a breath, considering what to say. "I know I've met someone pretty incredible. I don't know what you're asking or what you're fishing for, but that girl in there, she doesn't deserve some guy dumping her and running. She's had that once, and I'm not the kind of guy who'd do it. I don't know what's going to happen tomorrow, but I'm not too inclined to just leave. So here we are."

He didn't know what to make of the way she was looking up at him, but she nodded and patted his bare chest. "Well, thought you should know about your bike. It was the least I could do, considering…" She pulled her hand away and stepped back, and the old floor creaked.

He took in the old carpet runner in the hallway as she turned and started to the stairs before looking back to him. He wasn't sure what it was, whether she was happy he was with her daughter or something else entirely. She was as much a mystery as this entire place was.

He listened to the creak of the stairs and was shaking his head when he stepped back into the room. JD was sitting up in bed, her hair a mess and her expression that of a woman who'd just been fucked—and well, at that.

"Who was that?" she asked.

He closed the door and flicked the lock again before striding over to the bed. She had to look up at him as he stopped right in front of her. "Your mom, to tell me my bike's here, so looks like we don't have to drive out to get it," he said.

He wasn't sure what else there was to say. He tried to get his head around her mom, her dad, and Ray. This town seemed so different from where he'd come from, and though it was still the same country, he suspected he'd never be comfortable with this way of life.

She said nothing for a moment, then let the sheet fall away from her breasts and rose up on her knees. He reached down and pulled her up so she was right against him, her arms around his neck. She kissed him again, and he let his hands linger on her, down her back, feeling all that softness as she pulled away.

"So does this mean you're getting on your bike and riding out of here?" she said.

It was the same thing her mom had asked, and he took in the hesitation as he ran his hand over her arm, which was still linked around his neck. She flicked her gaze up to him, and the only thing he wanted to do was lie back down and bury himself in her again. There was something about her. Just one taste wasn't enough.

He shook his head. "Only if you're with me," he said before leaning down and pressing his lips to hers.

She pulled back, her arms still around his neck. "So after everything, yesterday, today, you still haven't left me. Why? I don't understand you, Chris."

He wondered whether she'd get it, that there was something so special about her—from her smile, to the light in her eyes, to the beauty that seemed to radiate from deep inside her. Something about her was so real that it touched him in a way no woman had before.

"There's something about you, JD," he said, "that makes me want to risk everything."

Chapter Thirteen

The room was hot—stifling, rather, even though there was air conditioning. JD was covered in a thin veil of sweat as she woke to see the late afternoon sun. She glanced over to Chris, who was naked and damp, stirring from where he had been asleep next to her after an afternoon of the best sex she'd ever had.

"What time is it?" she asked, hit by a wave of panic as she remembered everything from the morning, from Ray's ridiculous charges to the fact that the entire town now likely knew she'd been caught naked as the day she was born, about to have sex with a guy who'd ridden into town only the day before on a badass motorcycle. It was scandalous.

She was also stuck on the fact that half the town would be coming in for dinner soon and there wouldn't be anything to serve. It was an icy splash of water, and she bolted upright. The bed creaked as her feet hit the floor, and Chris stirred and groaned as he reached for his phone. She was looking for her clothes, her underwear, picking through the pile on the floor.

"Almost four thirty," Chris said, his deep voice groggy, that of a man who was satisfied and not ready to wake up. "Come back to bed."

She stepped into her underwear and pulled on her lacy bra with its plunging C cups. "No way! I didn't realize it was so late. I must've fallen asleep. There's the matter of dinner to cook. If it isn't ready when folks show up, then…" Well, she didn't know what to think, considering this had never happened before. The shock of knowing what everyone would think of her was making her act crazy.

Before Chris, her life had been…boring?

"Oh shit, oh shit…" She jammed her hands in her hair, feeling the tangles. The bed creaked when Chris slid out, leaving the sheets and blankets in a heap. She reached for her sundress on the floor with his shirt and pulled it over her head.

"I told you your mom was here," he said. "She knows where you are. Won't she take care of…?"

Maybe it was the expression on her face that had him stopping midsentence. Her heartbeat kicked up again.

"Right," he said. He reached for his jeans and pulled them on, and she noted he didn't seem to wear underwear. "You can put me to work, then. I'll give you a hand with whatever you need done."

She searched out her sandals and took a look in the mirror by the bathroom, seeing her hair, a tousled mess. She ran her fingers through it, trying to restore order, but her face said it all: With the color in her cheeks and her pink and swollen lips, there was no hiding from anyone that she'd been thoroughly and well fucked all afternoon. The horror of the moment finally sank in as she glanced back at Chris, who had his T-shirt on and was shoving his feet into sneakers.

"You look fine. Let's go," he said. As he pulled the door open, his gaze swept over her from her breasts to her toes. The way he watched her was so intimate and lingering, and he made a noise of appreciation as her feet started moving toward him as if they had a mind of their own, being pulled to him as if by a magical cord.

His hand slid around her, over her ass, pulling her right against him, and he leaned down and pressed a kiss to her lips in a way that seemed so damn possessive. He wasn't a man who asked, she realized. He took, and he did, and he seemed to understand what she wanted, what she needed. That kiss alone, as he tasted her again, was filled with such heat that he could have pulled her back to bed and she'd have gone willingly, wantingly, but she couldn't.

He broke the kiss, and she had to press her hands to his chest, so glad his arms were around her and holding her up, as her legs seemed likely to give way. She fisted her hands in his shirt, as she once again felt out of breath. It was what he did to her. His hand was sliding over her ass, feeling all of her. She'd never before felt so exposed, open, and vulnerable with a man, not even Matt.

She blinked away that image, as Chris seemed to just want to linger there, holding her. The way his eyes lazily waited for her to move or say something as they stood in that open door, she was hit with wonder at what a lifetime would be like with a man like him. It would be more than she could imagine.

She forced that image away. Reality awaited.

"We should go. I should go," she said, having to fight to get the words out.

A slow smile touched his lips, and he stepped back and reached for her hand, pulling her into the dimly lit hall, with its dark wood and long rug of mixed green and brown. She was seeing the lodge through Chris's eyes as she followed him out and pulled the door closed. They made their way to the stairs hand in hand, walking as close as they could, down each step, one foot and then the other. Her legs were still so weak, just like all of her body, sated and relaxed, so deeply relaxed.

She craved to just curl up with Chris, her arms and legs entwined with his. Her body needed to touch him. His hand slid around her back, her hip, as hers went around his waist, and they continued down the creaking stairs.

Then she saw them. At the bottom were people, and not just any people—her family.

It wasn't until Chris pulled her to a stop that she took in who was in front of her, waiting by the front desk, the opening to the dining room: her father, her mother, Ray, and even her grandparents, along with Judge Henry, a friend of her father's, the man whose signature was on her annulment with Matt.

For a second, she felt as if she were being dragged through time, reliving something she'd never wanted to experience again.

"What's going on?" she said. She could feel Chris tense, tightening his hold on her, as she took in everyone's mixed reactions. Her heartbeat kicked up.

"JD, it would be best if you went with your mother," her dad said.

This was déjà vu. Hadn't he said exactly the same thing four years earlier? Now here she was, reliving the same pattern. All of the fears she thought she'd buried long before suddenly exploded inside her. This was her father's heavy-handedness, and she recognized the possibility that this could be the last time she saw Chris. He'd stayed so far, but every man had a breaking point.

She shook her head and stood her ground. "No."

"It's fine, JD," Chris said as he moved in front of her,

looking down at her, both hands on her arms, holding her and rubbing as if to reassure her. He seemed so big and strong in that moment, but then, so had Matt. "It's okay. I'm not—"

She pressed her hand to his mouth. He had his back to her family, and she realized he didn't seem worried at all. There was something wrong with him. She feared never seeing him again. Didn't he get that?

"No, I'm not going anywhere," she said, then pulled her hand away and rested it on his chest. She stepped around him and faced everyone, and she felt his hands on her, as if he wasn't about to let her handle this alone. She wondered whether he knew what that meant, feeling as if he had her back.

"I'm not taking one step out of here after what happened this morning with Ray," she said, "after what you tried to do to Chris. It was so wrong." She jabbed her hand to the man who'd been her closest friend. The way he was staring at her, he was making her feel as if she'd betrayed him when she'd done nothing of the sort. "I mean, here we go, a total repeat. I can't believe I'm right back here, or so it feels. I don't understand what this is. You want me to leave and walk out of here so you can… what, threaten to charge Chris with some crime so that when I come back out later, he'll be packed up and gone? I don't understand what this is."

"JD," Chris said. His hands slid over her shoulders. He was holding her tight, and she felt the caring as he turned her to face him again. "It's okay. Nothing's going to happen."

How could he sound so damn confident? Even she was seeing what was going on. Her eyes were wide open now, her hands fisted, and she was ready to slug someone, she was so angry. She couldn't help the need. She pushed at his chest and stepped back, and his hands fell to his sides.

"Of course it will," she snapped. Something in his expression made her think he didn't understand. Or maybe he did.

"I'm not going to disappear," he said. "There's nothing anyone can say to me that would have me walking out the door and away from you. It's not going to happen."

The way he said it, she almost believed him, except she'd lived this very same thing. There were so many parallels.

But Chris wasn't Matt, and she wasn't a stupid, starry-eyed, naive teenager anymore.

"Oh, Jorden, you need to stop this," her grandmother said. She was wearing a silky bright orange and cream kaftan that went to her ankles, and her white hair still had marks from the rollers she wore at night. Her face was coated with a heavy hand of makeup as if she'd just been pulled from a game of bridge or any of the other afternoon activities she did with her group of retirees. Then there was her grandfather, who was an older version of her father. He sat there stoic, unsmiling, and said nothing.

"Really, Jorden, your mom is right," her mom said, her makeup flawless and her hair perfectly groomed. "You need to stop this nonsense. It's not like JD is still a teenager and has done something so stupid that she needs you to rectify it."

Her dad pulled off the ball cap he'd worn over his shaved head since his hair had thinned ten years earlier. It was always that and his badge, pinned to his chest, that she saw first and foremost. It was who he was. "I told you it's time she settled down," he said, gesturing to her mom as if they were having a private conversation about her, as if she had no say in her life, the same conversation they'd had before.

Ray said nothing from where he lingered.

She found herself searching out the door to the lodge, wondering why the restaurant was so quiet. She wasn't sure what she heard from Chris behind her, but she looked from her dad, to Ray, to her mom, and over to her grandma, who was rolling her eyes. She still didn't know why the judge was there, sitting at a table behind everyone in his dark pants and white shirt, the sleeves rolled up to show his thick arms. He had white hair, a mustache, and a face that was always free of emotion. Then there was her grandfather, who seemed to be taking in the scene as if he'd been told to come and watch. She never knew what was going through his head, what he'd say, what he'd do.

"Time to settle down… Did you really just say that?" JD said. "I'm not sure what this is or what this little gathering is about."

Her father was paying her no mind, she realized. In fact, he was staring across the room to Chris. The look, his expression, had a chill going up her back. "You say there's nothing that'll have you packing your bag and leaving, yet you took my daughter to your room and had fun with her all afternoon, carrying on as if she were a two-dollar hooker."

JD thought her grandmother groaned, and she knew her jaw dropped.

"And look at her," Jorden continued. "The way you two came swaggering down the stairs, you seem to think you can just roll into town, snap your fingers, and have my daughter at your beck and call, up in your room for an afternoon romp. Disrespectful is what you are. Right under my roof!"

She didn't know what to say. She stared in horror, realizing her father was talking about her sex life. To make it worse, he'd just reduced her to some trollop, as if she made a habit of throwing herself at men who stayed in their family lodge, selling herself. This was worse than anything, yet Chris still hadn't pulled his hand away from her. It was gripping her hip, holding her against him.

"That's not fair, Dad," she said, "and not true."

"Isn't it?" He snapped his gaze to her, freezing her where she was.

"I'm not sure what you're seeing," Chris said, "but JD isn't like that, and there was no disrespect. I care for JD very much."

Her dad let out a sharp, chilling laugh, one she knew was meant to intimidate whomever he was at odds with. "Really? How noble of you. Somehow, though, I think you may have a change of heart in a few seconds, because before this day is out, we're going to be having ourselves a wedding."

Chapter Fourteen

Chris had never been known to walk away from anything. His friends and family commented that he always stuck to his ideas with the kind of grit and stubbornness that would give a mule a run for its money. However, standing in the parlor of the lodge in Martin, in front of these people, the strangest family he'd ever encountered in his life, he was at a complete loss for words. In fact, he thought the floor may have softened under his feet.

He realized this game of roulette had started the moment he'd been pulled over outside town by the sheriff and his deputy, who were far from the type to ever back down, and it was now taking an unlikely turn.

"I'm not sure I understand…" Was that his voice?

JD was absolutely silent. He couldn't see her face, but he could only assume she was as thrown as him, or maybe she was used to her father pulling this crazy-ass shit.

Everyone seemed to be talking and arguing, and Chris had a sick feeling about what this all meant. Ray had done nothing but stare at JD the entire time with angst and emotion—nothing Chris liked. That kind of love from afar often ended badly, and worse, he realized, it had likely brought about this three-ring circus.

He didn't know who the other people were in back, an older couple and another guy who was dressed neatly and scribbling something on paper. He had yet to say one word.

"I'll marry her."

Chris heard it spoken softly, and he was staring at Ray even before anyone else realized the man had said anything. Ray was holding his hat in his hand, working it with his fingers, sitting on the velvet green settee and leaning forward, his arms resting on his knees. Everyone stopped talking.

Ray cleared his throat, sat up, and stood as if ready to make a declaration. "If you'll have me, JD, I'd make you a good husband. I think you know that, and we've known each other a long while, a good many years. I'll treat you well and look after you." He gestured to her, and Chris could feel JD stiffen against him.

"Well, there's one offer on the table," Jorden said, his thick hand in the air as if he were at an auction. Chris was about to laugh until he realized the man wasn't joking. No one was.

"Daddy, you can't be serious," JD said, sounding… well, he wasn't exactly sure. Her voice was strained.

"Oh, I'm very serious. I've had about enough of all of this. And especially of you," the sheriff said, pointing at Chris, "coming in here and disrespecting my daughter, my family, having her doing things she'd never do if she hadn't been led astray by the likes of you."

Chris just stared at the man, who was shooting daggers his way, and he realized Jorden saw him as someone responsible for the wrongs in this world, this very small-town world in South Dakota. It was unsettling to be slotted into that category, and he'd never have admitted to anyone how unnerved he was.

He took in the shotgun leaning against the wall behind the sheriff and realized each place he'd seen in this country —his country, with all its states, counties, and towns—was different from the next. All the people and places he'd once felt the need to see, understand, and experience had left him with one big question: Why? What had made following that curiosity seem like such a great idea?

And now what? He felt as if he'd stepped into another time, another place, another country, and he found himself searching for something in the room that would indicate he was, in fact, still in the USA.

"Ray," Jorden said, gesturing to the deputy, who just nodded, holding his Stetson, black brushed cowhide, against his leg. "JD, this is happening. You are our only daughter. It's not like this is your first time. Far from it. There was that other fellow who showed you he wasn't good enough for you, and now there's this one."

He gestured to Chris. "You, boy, are toying with my daughter and stirring up all kinds of talk in this town. You've thumbed your nose at my authority, showing everyone that it's just fine to undermine me and the law here, and that I can't have. Won't have. It will not happen. So listen up. A few things are about to happen here. JD, you've had one offer from a man you know has my approval. Your behavior shows you need to settle down. It's time, honey, that you had a family, set some roots in the community with someone who's already here, a respectable man who has this community's best interests in mind and is already a part of our family. He's our people."

Chris wasn't sure what to say as he listened to the sheriff, who seemed to think he could dictate JD's life and arrange it how he saw fit.

"Have you lost your mind?" JD said, an edge of panic in her voice. "Mom, Grandma, do something!"

All Chris could do as he took in everyone in the room was try to assess where they stood and just how far they'd be willing to go to take JD from him and see that she was hitched to the one man she didn't want. His gaze kept landing on that shotgun.

Her mother, Alice, who he'd thought was in their corner, only shook her head. "JD, I'm all for fun and everything, but I think this time your father is right. I may not agree with his approach, but I can see his point."

What the hell?

The older woman in the kaftan was staring daggers at the sheriff, though, and for a second Chris considered just maybe she might side with them, stand up, and put an end to this craziness. Someone had to be the voice of reason.

She remained sitting as she said, "I don't agree with my son. Let the girl have her fun. The only ones who've stirred things up with the town are you two." She flicked her hand to Ray and the sheriff. So that was JD's grandmother, the sheriff's mother, and the man beside her was likely her husband. He was trying to see a resemblance past the caked-on makeup, but he couldn't make one out. Her eyes were lined with black, and she had thick long lashes that seemed artificial.

Chris knew he needed to say something instead of letting everyone decide JD's fate, but he couldn't get his tongue to move. As JD turned to him, he could see her wild-eyed panic, as if she expected him to do something, say something in all this craziness to bring sanity and reason back to everyone.

"JD is not marrying Ray," he said. He looked at the

man he realized he'd been playing a very dangerous game with. "You may not like the fact that I'm here, and you've done everything in your power to try to drive me out of town and away from your daughter, but it hasn't worked. I'm still here. I also told you I'm not about to just get on my bike and leave without her."

He wasn't sure what he was seeing or feeling, but he knew he needed to find a way to end this now before it turned into something beyond what he could imagine.

The stern man in the back stood up as if he hadn't heard a word, paper in hand, and walked over to JD's grandparents. He set the page in front of them. JD's grandmother made a face as she looked up to him, and her husband nudged her as the man held a pen out to her.

"You can't make me get married to Ray," JD said, jamming her hands in her hair. "There's no way this is going to happen."

He could feel her energy spike as if she wasn't far from freaking out. They were doing everything they could to pull JD away from him. This had to be another game to mess with him. But although Chris was pretty intuitive and sharp, he was starting to feel as if this was beyond him, and he could very well find himself at the end of that shotgun, forced to ride out of town.

"You're right. They can't make you marry Ray," he said, his hand sliding around her hip, holding her close. He stepped around her and in front of her, and he didn't miss the way her mother's brow crooked. That appreciation he'd seen before in her expression was back, whatever that was worth. "This isn't going to happen. She doesn't want you. She made her choice," he said to Ray before dragging his gaze over to the sheriff.

Her father reached for the shotgun leaning against the wall and stepped over to the table where JD's grandparents were sitting. Chris's heart started hammering long and loud in his ears, because what the hell was he planning on doing with that gun?

"You witnessed, Mom, Dad?" the sheriff asked them.

"We did," the man answered, his voice deep and unsympathetic.

JD's grandmother was giving a withering, unimpressed look to her son. "Still don't agree with this, and not sure how you think this is going to happen, Jorden. It's one thing to rearrange JD's life, which you've done since she was a little girl, but she isn't one any longer. She doesn't need you to micro-manage and dictate how she's to live. And telling her who she's to marry?" She just shook her head.

Chris had to fight the urge to back her up. Maybe she was the voice of reason Jorden Cayhill needed to hear to end this insanity. He felt JD being pulled away from him even though she was right there, holding on to his arms. He could feel her trembling.

The sheriff said nothing, though his expression said his mind was set. He wasn't about to consider for a second what his mother was saying. He turned back to Chris and JD and then looked over to Ray, lifting the paper in the air until Chris could see the bold script at the top, *Marriage Certificate*. He took in each person in the room as his fingers dug into JD. This was suddenly far too fucking real for him.

"You see, only one thing is going to happen here," the sheriff said. "There will be a wedding, at which one of you will be marrying my daughter. Now, whose name goes at the top of this certificate is anyone's guess entirely. Is it going to be you?" He flicked the paper and jabbed it, pointing with his long, thick finger at Chris, then glanced over to Ray. "Or will it be my deputy, who's already thrown his hat into the ring? Just so we're clear and on the same page, Ray has my approval, whereas you, shithead, have done nothing but be a huge pain in my ass and cause me endless amounts of grief."

Then her father did something he hadn't expected: He walked past him and JD over to the front door. Just then, a young uniformed officer he'd never seen before came down the stairs carrying a bag—his bag! He set it down in the open doorway, and a confident smile touched the edges of the sheriff's lips. Chris didn't have a clue what this was, but it could be nothing good. He half expected hands to grab him and drag him out of there.

"Your bag has been packed," the sheriff said, "as I'm sure this is all too real for you, boy! Go on now and we'll forget all about this mess you've created. This is your chance to walk away free and unencumbered. It's your get-out-of-jail-free card, so run along and take it."

"Dad, what the hell are you doing?" JD was shaking from fear or anger at this crazed show. "This is too much. You've gone too far this time—"

"I'll marry her," he said, cutting JD off, having heard the panic in her voice.

For a second, he wasn't sure he'd said it. He was staring at JD's shocked expression. She seemed angry. He wanted to pull her aside even though her mother was glaring at him as if he'd completely lost it. Everyone in the room was silent, and uneasy exchanges were happening, as if Chris had changed the script. A certain outcome was becoming something none of them had expected.

Her father just stood there, not a smile on his face, and glanced over to the cop behind Chris. Now he was pretty sure he'd either be thrown out of town or maybe be put in jail again—and this time he wouldn't get out.

Chapter Fifteen

Her father had lost his mind, JD realized as she stared from Ray to Chris. She stood in the middle of the room, and Chris let his hand fall away from her shoulder, from touching her, which he'd been doing since they'd stepped out of his room. Now she wished they were still up there.

"There's no way I'm getting married," she said. "There's no way you can make me get married or have me agreeing to marry anyone. There is such a thing as free will. I actually have rights in this current day, and—"

Her mother stepped over to her, grabbed her wrist, and yanked her toward their rooms at the back of the lodge.

"Mom, let me go!" She couldn't believe how strong her mom was, and then another hand was on her shoulder. Her grandma? Seriously, both were dragging her out of there.

"You just hush up now, JD," her mother said, "and we're going to have a little talk."

She'd never heard her sound so mad, and she took in

Chris, who was left standing by the open door with the officer and Ray. They were all watching and not saying a word. She was humiliated, embarrassed, and couldn't believe this was happening.

"Grandma, talk some sense into everyone," JD said as her mom pulled her through the door into their comfortable living room, decorated in fashionable greens and whites, with artwork along the staircase that led up to her parents' master suite. Her room was straight ahead.

She heard the door behind her close and a lock click, and she turned to see her grandma standing there, looking a far cry from her days in the kitchen. She'd really taken her retirement fun to heart with the makeup, the outfit.

"So we won't be disturbed," she said. "I'm sure we've all had enough of my pig-headed son's heavy-handedness."

Great, a voice of reason! JD was about to go over and hug her.

Then her grandma said, "But, and I hate to say it, I agree with them."

What? She couldn't get her mouth to move. "How can you both stand by and assume I'd just pick a guy and get married? In case you both don't realize, I kind of like Chris, but that doesn't mean I want to get married right now." No, for the love of God, she'd just met him, and she was enjoying this, just being with him, getting to know him, and possibly looking forward to forever down the road, not that she was about to share that part with anyone.

"Maybe so, JD," Alice said, "but I think this little spectacle wasn't so much to get you married but to force Chris to give up and walk away. I guarantee you, never in a million years did your dad expect that boy out there to step up. Even I can't believe he said he'd marry you." Her mom was pacing the room, her arms crossed, and appeared far from together.

In fact, she couldn't remember her mom ever appearing so on edge, including the time her father had forgotten all about her birthday. For some, that would've been no big deal, but not for her mother. It had been akin to the end of the world, and it had taken her father eight very long weeks to dig himself out of that hole and get back in her good graces. "And just so there's no misunderstanding, I like Chris, I do, and he's especially easy on the eyes, but even I have to admit, marriage with a guy like that…" Her mom shook her head.

Her heart was sinking again. "Regardless of that little fact, which I can't believe we're even discussing, or the fact that Dad seems to have lost his mind and has Judge Henry here as if he can make me…" She had to stop to catch her breath, as she was shaking from the fury pounding at her over and over in waves. "Mom, I have feelings for Chris, whereas the only feelings I have for Ray are as a friend, nothing more. Until now, I never stopped to think that Ray would assume we'd get married or that something would happen between us. Even with all the hint-dropping by you and Dad, and Ray showing up to take me out, I just assumed it would never go that far. My bad for being so idealistic. But seriously, when we put all that aside, Chris has been subjected to unbelievable, horrible, awful crap from Daddy since the minute I drove up behind him and Ray to find him cuffed, lying out on that scorching blacktop. And this…this…" She lifted her hand and turned to see the heavy look leveled her way by her grandma. "This is like some frickin' backwoods soap opera."

"Just so you know, JD," her grandma said, "there are some things about my son that make me want to pull him aside and give him a good talking to, and this is one of them. I don't expect my son had any idea that your young man out there would actually step up and offer to marry you. I guarantee you Jorden was expecting him to be out the door, on his bike, and out of the county by now, never to come back." Her grandma lifted her hands as if at a loss for words, then actually laughed.

"I never in a million years expected what just happened," Alice said. "With all the props there, Judge Henry, the shotgun, Ray, and even that blank certificate, I guarantee you it was all for show—a very dramatic show to scare the ever-living shit out of that young man of yours, and honestly, any young man with a lick of sense would already be out the door and across the county line. We'd have seen the last of him, and that would've been that." She pressed her hands to her cheeks. She was flustered, and her mom didn't get flustered.

"So are you saying that big show of force out there was just that, a show to scare Chris away, and nothing else?" she said, looking from her mom to her grandma, who just shrugged.

"Yes," Alice said. She was pacing again, and her heels clicked in her wedged sandals. "If Chris had just done what your father expected, that would've been that. He was supposed to leave, and yet he's offered to marry you. I can't believe it. My, my, that young man has definitely won a spot in my heart." She sounded almost dreamy.

"So then Ray and all he said about…" She didn't want to say it, as she was still reeling from his heartfelt declaration about making a good husband for her. She cringed still at the shock of him saying it, thinking it.

"Was a total surprise," her mom said, and her grandma gestured as if she agreed. "I didn't expect Ray to say what he did, even though we all knew how much he cares for you. It seems everyone is going off script."

"So now what?" JD was still freaking out, because Chris had done the one thing she'd never expected.

"Well, for one," her grandmother said, "I do believe my son's idiotic plan just backfired and blew up in his face."

Her mom's face was grim and set, and she wasn't smiling. Where exactly did she stand?

"So what does that mean?" JD said. "One of you is going to go out there and get Daddy to see reason, back off of Chris, and leave us be, and we'll go on with our day as if none of this craziness happened?"

Her mother shook her head, and her grandmother stepped over to her. She too had a look that made JD's stomach bottom out.

"Well, therein lies the problem, JD," her grandmother said. "Too many people have seen my son force his hand today, and it'll be all over town if he were to leave you both be and back down. It's the same as a gun fight. Now, if he doesn't follow through, he'll forever be labeled a coward and be known as a man who can't even keep his daughter under control. The good folks would lose faith in him, and he'd be out come next election. He would lose control of the town now, and my son has no intention of stepping down or allowing his authority to be undermined in any way."

JD wasn't sure what her grandmother was saying, so she turned to her mother.

"You can't play this game with your father, JD," Alice said. "You've already seen how far he'll go with that near miss at the station. The charges for that nuisance misdemeanor were nothing. Yes, you made him back down with your very embarrassing public display, which, by the way, everyone in town is talking about, but as much as I'd like to support you in wanting to have time to get to know that young man, your time is up. Either you're going to go out there and tell him to go, or you're going to have to marry him."

She couldn't believe what her mom had said, and maybe Alice thought she was going to argue more, as she stepped forward and touched both her arms with her hands.

"You know what, JD?" she said. "There's one thing I know about your father, about men, and that's that when it comes to a woman, they rarely think rationally or consider the consequences of their actions. It's likely, more than likely, that Chris could find himself in a heap more trouble than he intended if you two were to thumb your nose at your father and refuse this. That's all I'm saying—and not that I know what the trouble would be, but I know that the way this is going, you need to ask yourself whether you can see a future with that boy out there or not. If not, you tell him to go. For his sake." Her mom was serious, and when she turned to her grandmother, she couldn't believe she was of the same mind. The way she inclined her head and the sympathy in her expression said so.

"This is kind of unusual, this whole thing, but that young man out there has gotten under your father's skin, and Ray's too," she said. "Don't think I've ever seen him this way. I suspect Ray thought he had time to woo you over and get you to see things his way, get you to fall in love with him. So your mom's right: Something could happen, and it could be anything. If Chris chooses not to walk, he could end up with a record, serving time. I don't think you want that."

She covered her face. If anyone had asked her the day before whether this was possible, she'd have said no, but after what Ray had done with the public indecency charges, she realized Chris could very well be stuck with one big headache all because of her. She could send him away, but just the thought of never seeing him again was almost too much.

"So I guess we're having a wedding," she said.

Chapter Sixteen

No one said a word. Chris patted the back pocket of his jeans but already knew his phone wasn't there. It had to have been thrown in his bag, which was still sitting just outside the open door, and the cop was blocking it so no one could go in or out. The sheriff and Ray were talking with the judge and JD's grandfather.

Whatever they were saying, he couldn't make it out, but he realized he was out of his depth regardless. He needed to call his brother, his dad, someone who could be a voice of reason and a sounding board to help him make sense of this farce, to help him out of this impossible mess.

Had he really said he'd marry JD? Yeah, he had, and now he realized his father had been right about a lot of things, including the very pertinent fact that he had a way of digging himself into problems. Then, instead of thinking his way out of them like a reasonable person would, he did the opposite, digging himself in deeper with his stubbornness. It was that part of him that just couldn't let anyone mess with him.

He turned, taking in the young cop, whose expression

was like granite and gave nothing away. He was about to say something and reach for his bag when he spotted JD, followed by her mother and grandmother. She'd changed into a simple peach and white sundress that stopped at mid thigh, and even her hair appeared neatly brushed. She stood just short of her father in the middle of the room, taking in all the men, and then lifted her chin.

"Well, shall we get on with this? Where do you want us, Judge?" she said but didn't look his way.

Chris thought he heard the deputy swear, or maybe it was him, and then her father was staring at him with a look that told him he would've been more than happy to put him in the ground. Maybe he still would.

"You can't be serious, JD," the sheriff said. "You're not going to marry him."

Chris was thinking he needed to get his phone and put a stop to this.

"You gave me an ultimatum," JD replied. "Ray, I'm sorry, but since there's no choice—as you indicated, Daddy —Chris and I…" She stopped talking and looked over at Chris, and he took in those deep amber eyes, which he'd been lost in only an hour earlier as he'd made love to her over and over upstairs.

He didn't have a clue what she was thinking, but he could feel her around him still, the touch of her, the smell of her. Did he want her again? Yeah, but the icy reality of the current situation had him wondering why he wasn't walking out that door. He was drawn to her still, but marriage… How could this be happening?

Oh, yeah. He'd just tossed the offer out there.

JD was looking at him, and he could see her confidence wavering. "Chris, you offered to marry me. Were you serious?" Her voice was shaky.

He needed to say no and pull her out of the room,

away from everyone, where they could talk alone and find a way out of this insanity. Maybe he could get her on his bike and ride the hell out of there. And then what?

"I'm a man of my word," he said before he could think. He lived and died by that, something his father had drilled into him. A man was only as good as his word. Damn him already for being so fucking honorable! He made himself pull in a breath past the tightness in his chest.

JD nodded, and he realized she was waiting for him to do something, so he stepped forward, another step, and then another, until he was beside her and reaching for her hand, feeling how cold it was, trembling even though it was so warm out. She sounded calm and certain, but he could feel she was far from it. She needed him to handle this, to do or say something.

"Well," Alice said, clapping her hands as if to snap everyone out of a lull, "unless you all want the dinner rush to show up while we're performing the wedding, I suggest we get this done."

JD's mother somehow herded the sheriff to one side, and her grandparents stood to the other. Then the judge took up a spot right in front of JD and Chris, whose heart hammered in his chest.

"Do you each have vows you want to say?" The judge looked to him and then JD.

He just blinked, without a clue what to say, because this couldn't be happening. He glanced to the side to see Ray standing there, far from happy. "No," he finally said.

JD muttered the same in a soft voice he could barely hear.

"Well, then I guess we'll do the simple version and get right to it," the judge said. "I'm going to need your full name for the record."

"Christopher Friessen." He could feel JD looking up at him.

"Christopher Friessen, we have witnesses here, so will you take Josephine Denise Cayhill to be your lawfully wedded wife?"

That was it? Seriously, his brother had been asked something much longer, and that was after the minister had gone on and on for what felt like forever. The vows had included things like love and respect and protection, he thought. The judge was waiting, and he could feel JD tense beside him.

"I do," he said and looked to JD, who let out a breath. Maybe she thought he'd say, *Oops, sorry, mistake, got to go!* But even though he was thinking that very thing, he'd never do that to her.

"JD, will you take this young man, Christopher, to be your husband?"

That was it. He was staring at her, and for a minute he didn't think she'd answer or agree. She'd likely tell them all that this was a mistake and she wasn't going through with it. Good, let her be the voice of reason. *Please!*

"I will," she whispered.

He took in the judge staring at her as if he wasn't sure she'd said it, but then he nodded.

Chris glanced over to the sheriff, who said nothing, though his gaze, which was settled now on him, said everything.

"Well, then by the power vested in me by the state of South Dakota, you are now husband and wife."

Chris jerked his head back to the judge, as there was no way it could be that fast. That was it, seriously? They couldn't really be married now, but the man ushered JD to the table and pointed to a spot with his stubby finger, and she picked up the pen and scribbled her signature. Then she turned and held the pen out to Chris.

He almost heard music playing as he took a step, the floor softening, and reached for it. Sweat was pouring down his back. He stared at the marriage certificate, which had been filled out and signed by witnesses beforehand. There was just one spot left to sign, and he couldn't help wondering, if he walked out now without signing, would they still be legally married? This was a farce, yet he'd agreed, so he took the damn pen, stared at the black line, and scribbled his signature. He tossed the pen down.

"I'd say that should do it," the judge said.

Chris stared over to JD, who appeared close to shell-shocked. She was looking down, and he didn't know what was wrong, but he knew she was far from all right and he needed to say something, something that would…what, make this better?

"It's going to be okay," he said, but the words fell flat even to his own ears as he rested his hand on her shoulder.

She looked up at him, staring at him not with the love or passion she'd had for him earlier but with something he hadn't expected: anger. She was furious at him, but how could that be? After all, he was the one who'd offered to marry her, and he had. If anyone should've been angry, had a right to be angry, it was him.

"Really, you believe that?" she said. Then she stepped back, turned away, strode back to the lodge where she lived, and slammed the door shut behind her.

Chapter Seventeen

There was a tap on her door, and she didn't turn around from where she sat perched at the edge of her unmade bed. Then she heard the familiar squeak of the old door as it popped open, and when she turned to see who it was, she didn't expect to see Chris standing there.

Her husband!

The surreal thought hit her. She couldn't believe they were married and he was still there. Why? She had so many questions as she stared at a man she barely knew.

He still hadn't said anything as he stepped inside her bedroom and shut the door. "So I kind of didn't expect that from you. What gives?" he said. She thought she picked up an edge to his voice.

Her fingers dug into the mattress as he stepped closer. How could he be standing there so calmly after what had just been forced upon them? None of this made sense.

"Why did you do it?" She sounded accusing even to her own ears. She hadn't meant to, or maybe she had. From his expression, she didn't understand what he was thinking. His face was hard, unfeeling, and none of his earlier charm was there. This was a stranger she didn't know, even though there was something about him that she wanted, needed, and was so attracted to that he'd been in her every thought.

"You're going to have to be a little more specific," he said. "I'm not sure what to say about the fact that we're now married. I'd always considered shotgun weddings to be from another time, but everything about Martin seems to be so…" There was no humor in his voice.

She just stared at him. He still stood against the closed door as if he had no intention of closing the gap between them. They were about as far apart as they could be, not just in terms of distance, especially after what had just happened. They were married!

Hadn't she been here before, in another time, with another man? Only then it had been her choice to be married, something she'd wanted, and her father had made sure to undo it all, showing her once again that he held all the power and would always run her life. She should be laughing because she'd just turned the tables on him, but she wasn't.

"You don't need to say it, Chris, that maybe you've had a chance to think about it and you know it was a mistake. I don't understand why you said you'd marry me, why you did it, why you went through with it when you and I barely know each other."

She wanted to love, to be loved, and she liked Chris, really liked him. Hell, the chemistry between them rocked so much that being with him was something she craved, and she wasn't ready to walk away from it. But now, after all was said and done, something else was settling between them. She stared at her bare fingers, where a ring should've been, but there had been no ring, no flowers, nothing to make the day special.

Chris let out an exasperated sigh that had her looking up at him. He rested his hand over the metal foot rail of her bed and took another step closer. She still didn't have a clue what was going through his mind. She took in his hand, which she'd felt running over her body and which had taken her places she'd never experienced with a man before. Then he was in front of her, and he slid his hand under her chin so she had to look up at him.

"JD," he said, reaching for her hand. "It is what it is. I said I'd marry you, and I mean what I say. I'm not one to go back on anything, and I'm not running out on you. Don't you think I can see it in your face, your expression? But then you suddenly turned on me out there. I don't get it."

He gestured outside, and she could see how he'd taken it. They really weren't on the same page about anything. He stepped back again, filled with passion and fire, and she sensed a man who couldn't be pushed into saying or doing anything he wasn't ready for. Yet he'd married her.

"I'm not the one who forced you to walk out there and go through with this," he said. "But, JD, if you're going to see me as the one who did something wrong here, as the bad guy…"

She stood up, right in front of him, seeing his anger, feeling it. She pressed her hand over his chest, to his arm, though she wasn't sure she had the right to touch him, and he sighed. "You know what?" she said. "This isn't what I expected, either. I'm sorry. I didn't mean to make you feel as if I'm angry at you. I just don't understand why you said it, why you offered to marry me."

Her hand was still pressed to his chest as she waited, feeling the pull of his breath, the beat of his heart. What was he thinking? What was going through his head? Those vibrant blue eyes gave not a clue, steeped in so much more emotion than she'd ever seen in anyone before. Would she ever get used to this man?

He slid one hand over hers, then ran his fingers through her hair with the other, pulling her closer so her breasts pressed against him. She was feeling every hard part of him, which stirred feelings in her that only confused her more.

"Because there's something about you, JD. Having another man standing in the background who wants you so badly that he's willing to go to any length to have you…" He stopped, and she just stared up at him, waiting for him to finish. "It wasn't going to happen," he said. "You didn't want him. You've made that clear, yet it seemed as if Ray was convinced that making you be with him was the way to get you. I had enough. I have no intention of walking away from you. He can't have you."

He leaned down and pressed his lips to hers in a light and tender kiss. Then he pulled back, his forehead to hers. His hands slid around her, over the small of her back, over her ass, pulling her closer to him, pressing her against him.

"Chris, what are we going to do?" she whispered.

There was a tap on her door, and she wanted to weep at the interruption and yell at whoever it was to go away. Hadn't everyone messed with her life enough for one day?

"JD, it's your mother."

She was surprised she hadn't walked in, but maybe Alice thought she and Chris were already stripped naked and in bed.

"What?" she called out, leaning her head back and looking to the door.

Chris stepped back again, and this time he went over to the door and pulled it open. She mourned the loss of him against her. They had a lot to figure out, to discuss, like where to live. Here? Somehow, she didn't think he'd agree. Then there were a whole lot of other things they had to figure out together, like jobs, housing, the future, or should they call it quits? Of course he'd want to. It was only reasonable.

The door was open now.

"JD, just wanted to tell you your grandma is sticking around to help with the dinner rush, so you and Chris can have the night off," Alice said as if this were just an everyday thing, and she smiled and actually patted Chris's chest. "Oh, and, Chris, Jorden would like to have a word with you. Right now."

Here it goes, JD thought, starting across the room to them. "Really, is this where Daddy does something to strong-arm Chris into leaving? No, sorry, but if Daddy wants to speak with Chris, I'm coming too. He's gone too far this time." She was furious and could feel the pulsing beat of her heart. As she took in Chris, his expression, she didn't know what he was thinking. Then there was her mother.

"JD, you need to have a little more faith in me," Chris said, touching her arm, holding her. "I'm not going anywhere. Said it before, and I mean it. Haven't you figured that out? If your father wants to have a word with me, fine, because I have some things I need to say, as well."

She wondered whether Chris ever gave in. What the hell was he thinking? Her father was not a man to be messed with. Hadn't he figured that out already? "Chris, I don't think that's a very good idea," she said, but she realized, as he shook his head and stepped around her mom, that he had a stubborn streak a mile wide. Something else about him that she was just figuring out.

He turned back in the doorway, facing her mom and

her. "It'll be fine, JD. I'll talk to your father, and then when I'm done, you and I need to figure some things out."

Then he was walking away, across the living room to the door that led out to the main lodge, and she just stared over at her mother, who was watching Chris with amusement and what seemed like appreciation.

Chapter Eighteen

Not only was his cell phone not in his bag, but said bag, which had been just outside the now closed front door to the lodge, was currently tossed on the settee where Ray had been sitting earlier. Chris grabbed it, climbed the creaking stairs, and strode back to the room he'd paid for. The door was sitting wide open, and the bed was now stripped as if someone was ready to make up the room.

He closed the door and dropped his bag on the bare mattress, not about to be summoned or dictated to by the asshole father he suspected was about to strong-arm him, threaten him, or maybe do something worse. Was some other twisted scenario about to come out of nowhere and smack him upside the back of the head?

He was starting to realize he needed to be one step ahead of the sheriff, a man who was now his father-in-law. That fucked-up thought had him hesitating as he rested his bag on the bed and rummaged. Fuck, no cellphone. It had to be there somewhere. He finally spotted it on the old wood dresser beside the bathroom along with his bike keys. Yes!

He grabbed the phone and powered it on to see three messages, then brushed back the sheer curtain and looked out to where his bike was parked out front, where JD's mother had said it would be. He was fighting the pull to get on and ride as he listened to the first message, from an hour ago.

"It's your brother. Remember I said to call me tonight? Well, I should have said exactly what time—like now, like right now. I've thought about why you called, about everything you said happened, and I can't shake this really, really bad fucking feeling, so call me now. Bye."

That was so Danny. He listened to the next, from his brother again, thirty minutes later.

"So, haven't heard from you, and it's not like you not to call back unless you decided to do the smart thing and get on your bike, ride the hell out of that town, and forget the babe. Seriously, I hope you suddenly regained some of those lost brain cells and you're somewhere close to the Washington border and are going to be home tonight."

The last message wasn't from Danny: "Hi, Chris, it's your mom. It's been a few days, and we just thought you'd be home by now. We miss you, love you, can't wait to see you. Give me and your dad a call when you get this."

Great. He tapped his head with his cell phone, walking away from the window. Not only did he have to check in with his family, but he needed to tell them what had gone down, and right now he wasn't looking forward to telling them about his wife or any of the details of that story. Was there any possible way he could sugarcoat any of it? Not likely.

Someone knocked on the door just as he lifted the phone, dialed, and listened to the first ring.

"Where the hell are you?" Danny snapped. "Seriously, tell me right now you're at some rest stop and are almost home, because Evie was just talking with Mom on the phone, and she said she hasn't heard from you for a few days. To make it worse, she said she has this feeling that something isn't okay. I swear Mom has some fucking ESP shit going on."

He just listened to his brother rant, staring at the door, which opened to reveal JD's father. He was Chris's height, with broad shoulders, a bald head, a strong jaw, and a round middle. He was a big man who carried weight and threw it around at the same time, which likely was what intimidated everyone around him.

"Hello! Chris, are you there?"

He had to pull the phone from his ear at his brother's yelling. "Yeah, sorry, Danny. Look, I just wanted to check in like I said I would, but something's come up and I've got to go," he said, ready to hang up and find out what the hell was coming at him now from the sheriff. That was another thing: Was he there as a father, as a sheriff, or as something else?

"No you don't! You're staying on the phone with me until I know what the fuck is going on," Danny said. "Are you still in Martin, or did you leave?"

Maybe it was rude to talk on the phone when someone was waiting. It was something his mother had always drilled into him, that manners mattered, politeness mattered, but right now the sheriff was pushing every one of his buttons.

"I'm still here, and there's something I need to talk to you about. This thing kind of snowballed and took a turn in a direction I didn't expect." Now he was being cryptic.

"Expect? Seriously, Chris, if this were anyone else, I'd brush it off, but you're one of the least dramatic people I know, the one who never worries about anything, and the most unwilling to share, so now I'm worried. Do you need me to come down there? I can call Dad. He could be there in…"

He heard what sounded like tapping on a desk, and he wanted to laugh, but the last thing he needed was his family showing up, because it would turn this situation into something untenable. Until he got a handle on it, he needed to see that they stayed away. He shook his head but knew his brother couldn't see him.

"No, but let me call you back in, say, half an hour and we can talk."

The sheriff was still staring at him. Anyone else wouldn't have been so intrusive or rude, but this man had already shown from the first moment Chris had encountered him that he wasn't the neighborly, friendly sort.

"Look, there's someone here, and I need to speak with him…" He gave the sheriff his back and stared out the window, slipping one arm across his chest and tucking it under his other arm, where his T-shirt was damp again. It was the heat this time of year, so damn hot in this room. "It's the sheriff, the father of the girl I was telling you about, which is something else I need to tell you—and Mom and Dad, actually."

There was silence on the other end. He knew the sheriff was staring at him. He could feel it in the tightness in his back. His mom had always teased him, saying he used his Spidey senses more than anyone.

"I kind of got married," he said, then turned around and faced the sheriff, wondering what he would say.

He didn't think Danny could get any quieter. Then he said, "Did you just say you got married?"

"Yeah, and I've got to go. I'll call you back. Oh, and

don't tell Mom and Dad just yet. It's better if they hear it from me."

Then he hung up before his brother could lay into him or question him about what part of his anatomy he was using or whether he'd had a head injury along the way and lost his mind. Chris tucked his phone in his back pocket.

"Just in case you're wondering, that was my brother, who's just finishing up law school," he said. "Oh, and my mom is also a lawyer." He didn't mention his dad, who wouldn't hesitate to get in the face of this sheriff and wouldn't let him walk away from all the shit he had just pulled. There'd be nothing Chris could say to stop him. No, Jed had taught his sons how to be men, real men, the kind of role model every young boy needed.

"I sent my wife to track you down so's we could have us a sit-down and discuss what my expectations are of you now," Jorden said.

It wasn't lost on Chris that the man was wearing his holstered gun as he rested his hands on his heavy belt over his hips, and it also wasn't lost on him that it seemed he didn't care who Chris's family was or the fact that they could cause him a serious amount of legal grief.

"Here I am," Chris said, knowing his father would likely have kicked him in the backside for sounding like an arrogant ass. "So what's this discussion you want to have with me?" he added, not really interested in making this easy for the man. From Jorden's expression, the hardness there, Chris could see he was succeeding in pushing his buttons.

"So what's your deal?" the sheriff said. "I mean, what is it you get out of marrying my daughter other than becoming a general pain in my ass?"

Oh, so there it was. If that were his main objective, he'd have been happy, but the fact was that he was now married to JD, and he couldn't quite figure out how to come to terms with this man, who was supposed to love his daughter but had treated her as if she were nothing but a pawn in some chess match.

"You're kidding, right? You're the one who orchestrated that sideshow downstairs. You likely had a different outcome in mind, like me being long gone and your daughter being married to your deputy. What gives with that? Seriously, the man is older than her by at least ten years, if not more, and JD doesn't see him as anything other than a friend. Then there's Matt."

Oh, that had the sheriff's attention.

"Yeah, your deputy told me," Chris said. "Paid me a visit one night. Found him waiting for me in my room. Told me all the gory details of how you blackmailed Matt with a past he never wanted JD to know, and you knew exactly what it would take to get him to walk away from her, to sign the annulment papers and never contact her again. I can't help thinking now, what is it that you have in store for me?

"I'm sure you've searched out everything about my past, dug up every rock, and likely know what banks I keep my accounts at, how much money I have, who I owe, what I own. Maybe if you're really persistent, you'll have learned about the time I tossed a rock at Abbigail Stringham, hitting her in the head, where she bled like a stuck pig. She was okay, mind you, but then, I was only five. Or maybe you want to know about all the detentions I served in grade six, eight, and ten, all because I was the kid who couldn't get along with a teacher who thought he knew everything but in fact knew nothing. I was a pain in the ass, but I'm also the kind of guy who doesn't let assholes like you run me out of anywhere or try to maneuver JD, who's now my wife, into anything she doesn't want to do."

Holy crap, had he really said all that?

The sheriff smiled. What the fuck? "You have your little fun," he said. "Get it all out of your system, and then let me tell you how things are going to work around here if you expect to stay married to my daughter."

Was he kidding? Hadn't he heard anything Chris had said? Likely not. It seemed the sheriff had an agenda, and he was sticking to it.

"First, Matt LaCroix was a goddamn little pissant who went after a seventeen-year-old girl, and he'd never have amounted to shit. The problem with JD is she's an idealist who's been sheltered, and Matt was an ex-con working a seasonal job on a cattle ranch, bunking with the hired hands and lowlifes. He would never be anything but second rate. You...frankly, I haven't figured out whether you're just stupid or so stubborn that you can't help digging yourself further into a hole a smarter man wouldn't have wound up in to begin with. Also, a word of advice: A smart man knows when it's time to cut his losses. Anyhow, you're here. You actually married my daughter." He stopped and took a breath, and Chris could feel his back stiffen, the muscles tightening across his shoulders.

"You and JD can stay downstairs," the sheriff continued. "The house in back is big enough. You move into her room and stay with her there. This up here is for paying guests. Oh, and last, you'll be required to contribute to the family with a job, something. So, Mr. Christopher Friessen, from North Lakewood, Washington, son of Jed and Diana Friessen, with two brothers, Mark, who's still at home in middle school, and Daniel, who's married to Evie Wetzel, living in a cramped Seattle studio suite while his wife waits tables at a downtown bar and he studies at law school, currently interning at King County..." He leaned forward, and his brows lifted. "You see? I do my homework, and I do it well. Didn't get where I am by taking chances and not figuring out who all the players are."

Instead of saying something that would land him in a lot more trouble, this time Chris kept his mouth shut.

"So here're your options, and you got one day to figure them out. You'll help JD out with this family lodge, but you'll also get yourself a job, a decent job, a real job. You come up with a plan for the future, and tomorrow, you and I are to sit back down and discuss it. I'll finetune it for you." He walked to the door and glanced back, his gaze going to Chris's open bag on the bed. "Oh, and a word to the wise, Chris: You'd better make sure my daughter stays happy." Then he stepped out of the room and tapped the doorframe once before glancing back and saying, "Enjoy your night."

What an odd thing to say. Chris listened to the sheriff's footsteps on the old creaking floorboards as he went down the stairs, whistling, and then he swiped his hand over his face and pulled his phone from his pocket, knowing the call he needed to make. At the same time, he didn't have a clue how to explain any of this craziness to Danny or to his mom and dad.

Chapter Nineteen

They'd covered roughly twelve hours of what was normally a two-day road trip on the back of Chris's bike. JD had sat with her arms wrapped around his waist, leaning against him, all day.

They had set out after their first night as a married couple, an awkward night spent in her room, where they'd actually just slept. She'd woken at dawn to find Chris sitting in a chair in the corner, already dressed, and all he'd said to her was "Pack a bag. We're leaving."

Knowing her parents were still asleep, she'd pulled on blue jeans and a T-shirt, shoved her feet into sneakers, and put on the jean jacket Chris grabbed out of her closet. He'd pulled her from the lodge, carrying her bag, then had her on the back of his bike, driving to meet his parents in North Lakewood. The only reason he'd given her was that it was best for them, both of them, to be out of her father's reach for now.

Something must have happened.

She tapped Chris on the back when she spotted a gas station up ahead. She needed to pee again, and she needed to stretch and move, get a coffee or something. Mostly, she needed him to talk to her. He pulled off, slowed, and pulled up to the pump, and she gripped his arm as she lifted her leg to get off.

He slid his cracked visor up as she unsnapped her helmet and lifted it off. She wished the charm and mischief she'd first seen in his blue eyes would look back at her now. As if he sensed her unease, he reached up and touched her chin, her cheek.

"Do you want anything inside?" she said, though she could see nothing edible through the window of the old and dingy gas stop.

He pulled off his helmet, then shook his head as he turned off the bike and propped the kickstand down. "Hey." He slid his hand over her arm, the leather of his jacket rustling as he held her wrist, and she could see the sweat on his forehead. "Just grab a water. We should be at my mom and dad's in a few hours, just before dark."

He was still holding her arm, and she couldn't resist reaching out and brushing at his chin, feeling the bad-boy look of a few days without shaving. She stepped in closer, tilting her head down, brushing over his lips. She didn't know why she needed the reassurance. It was a quick kiss, but it was filled with none of the earlier tension.

Chris had barely said anything, and the fact was that she was still reeling from what had happened the day before. She knew he'd had a talk with her father, but he'd shared nothing. In fact, he'd become distant and moody. She didn't know how to deal with distant and moody Chris.

She nodded and then patted her pocket, but she didn't have cash. Maybe he understood, as he stood and opened the compartment of his gear where he'd stuffed his wallet. He pulled out a ten and handed it to her, and she hesitated just a second before taking it, looking up at a man she had to remind herself she was married to, a man she didn't know the first thing about.

"My wallet's in my bag," she said.

He didn't reply for a second. Then he said, "You're my wife, JD, my responsibility. I don't need or want your money."

She didn't know what to say, and she wasn't sure how to take what he'd said. They needed to sit down and talk about everything, including what her father had said to him. Chris just wasn't one to share anything.

She nodded. "You know I don't expect you to pay my way, and I'm still not sure about all of this. Chris, I left my mother a note..." she said, thinking of her, feeling horrible.

As she looked up at him, she didn't understand his expression. He looked past her, and she remembered what he'd said, that they were going to his parents' place and she could call her parents then. That was all the information he had given her before pulling her out of the home she'd been born in, where her father had been born and his father before that. It was as if she'd left everything of who she was behind, yet he still didn't seem willing to tell her what was going on.

His hand was on her cheek, his thumb caressing, and it was this that made her feel as if she meant something to him, yet at the same time, he didn't share anything of who he was or what he was thinking.

"Chris, you still haven't told me what my dad said and why you felt the need to sneak out before everyone was awake. It makes me think something happened between you, which, knowing my dad and what's happened thus far, is likely. Did he threaten you?"

He finally pulled his hand away and looked over her

head again, his expression completely unreadable. She was so damn hot, and her shoulders ached and pulled. She didn't know how he'd ridden cross country on a bike for months. His red hair was a mess, but his messy look was so fucking sexy. Add in his solid abs and broad shoulders, and he carried himself like a rock. She realized he wouldn't take shit from her dad or anyone.

"JD, your dad is the kind of guy who has to have things his way, no matter the cost. We weren't going to stick around another moment, waiting for the other shoe to drop. No one tells me what to do or runs my life. Besides, we need to figure some things out, and it won't happen in Martin. I wasn't leaving you there."

For a minute, she wasn't sure what to make of that. Maybe that was what he saw in her face when he kissed her again and then patted her ass as if to move her along.

"I've got to gas up," he said. "Go to the bathroom, get us some water. I don't want to linger any longer than we have to."

Then he was unscrewing the gas cap and shoving in the nozzle to fill the tank. When he turned back to her, though, she was still standing there. It seemed that although Chris was different from her father in so many ways that mattered, the man she had married was actually as secretive, strong, demanding, and set in his ways as Jorden Cayhill was.

Chapter Twenty

Driving through Arlington in the dark, he could feel the pull home. He gave the bike more gas, blowing through North Lakewood and seeing the miles disappear, the familiarity becoming a giant ache in his chest. It had been so long, over three months, and as he drove down the long dirt driveway to his parents' home, the huge barn, the arenas, and the corrals appeared larger the closer he got.

JD's hands tightened around him. The house was dark as he pulled in and parked, and he needed to take a second, seeing the light on in the loft above the barn. Danny's Bronco was there, and his dad's truck, and his mom's SUV. Being home created such an ache that for a moment, he was furious at the mist he had to blink back.

He turned off his bike as he heard the squeak of a door, and he pulled off his helmet. JD climbed off the back, her hands still on him. His mom was coming down the steps. He felt gritty, needing a hot shower.

"You're home," Diana said. Her red hair was longer now, messy, and she was wearing a silky long dark robe. Of course they'd been asleep, as he assumed it had to be close to midnight. Then there was his dad, barefoot and bare chested, wearing only jeans. They were looking at JD with hesitation and confusion, and he knew they were waiting for him to explain.

"Hello, I'm JD," she said when he didn't. She pulled off her helmet and tucked it under her arm as Chris got off the bike.

"JD, it's nice to meet you," Diana said, reaching for her hand. She had a way of making everyone feel welcome, but she was still looking to him to explain.

"JD," Jed said, reaching around Diana to shake JD's hand. "This is quite a surprise. Didn't know you were coming in tonight, Chris. Should've let us know," he added, taking in his son.

Chris spotted movement by the barn, a flashlight on the ground, and there was his brother Danny, with Evie beside him, really digging into the dirt. The door to the house opened, too, and he spotted Mark, his bright red hair a mess. Chris rested his helmet on the seat and walked around to stand by JD, sliding his hand over her back.

"Hey, Christopher, you made it back," Mark said, looking at his bike with a lot of envy. He knew his younger brother had been jealous of the fact he'd up and rode off to see a big chunk of the country. It was something Mark would've loved to do. Then there was Danny, who was staring at JD and then him, and Chris knew he'd stayed true to his word and not said a thing to his parents.

"Danny, when did you get here?" Chris asked.

"A few hours ago," Danny replied, looking down at JD. "Danny, the older brother," he added, holding out his hand to her.

"JD," she said.

Evie also gave him a look before shaking JD's hand. So

polite, and he knew there were questions everyone was evidently not going to ask.

"So, everyone, this is JD," Chris said. "You've all met her now, and you're likely wondering what's going on. Well…she's my wife."

Yeah, he could have handled that better.

He didn't know why he looked over to Mark, who seemed the only one happy at the news. His mom and dad were staring at him as if they didn't have a clue who he was or what to say, and Danny appeared awkward as he shook his head and ran his hand over his neck, giving him a pointed look.

"Seriously, Chris?" he said.

"Married, you got married?" Diana said, looking from him to JD.

His dad was staring at him in a way that let him know he had a few things to say. Chris could feel the tension, the awkwardness, and for a moment he wondered whether Danny had said something, after all.

"We should go in, everyone," Jed said, gesturing to the stairs. "Danny, Evie, JD, come on. It's late."

Chris watched as his mom started up the steps. She'd somehow maneuvered JD and Evie ahead of her, Mark following behind.

As Chris unfastened the bags from his bike, his dad rested his hand on top of them, stopping him. "Married, seriously? I have a feeling there's a story or something. Am I right?" he said. Then he shook his head as he took one of the bags, hefting it as if it weighed nothing, not pulling his gaze from his son.

He knew how well his dad could read him, all of them. He wanted to look away, but he didn't, instead reaching for the other bag. Then he looked over to Danny, who only lifted his hands and shook his head.

"I didn't say anything," he said, "but Mom and Dad were thinking something was up."

Jed stopped where he was. He'd seen that look on his dad's face only a time or two, growing up. "So you knew, then," he said to Danny. He didn't need to raise his voice.

"I called Danny and told him," Chris cut in, knowing his dad wouldn't be brushed off, "but I also told him not to tell you and Mom, as I needed to do that. I needed to tell you I got married and what happened."

Even Danny didn't know all the details, he realized.

"Hmm," his dad said, taking him in again. "Can't wait to hear this." Then he started up the stairs and pulled open the door. He hadn't gone soft in the middle, Chris noted, but his chest hair wasn't as dark as it used to be, from what he could tell from the outside light. He was still carrying JD's bag as he said, "Come on, you two."

Chris stepped inside, taking in the familiar entry. Something about being in the home where he'd been born and grown up had him breathing a lot easier. Everything was the same, but he was so different. He looked around at the small living room with a sectional and an easy chair, which opened to the dining area, where there was a table for six, and the tiny boxy kitchen, which had never changed, then to the back of the house, which his dad had added years ago, where the family room and his room were. It was cozy and comfortable, and he couldn't wait to put his head on the pillow and sleep—with JD. Right, he really needed to figure out everything and how JD would fit.

She was sitting on the sectional, and Evie was in the easy chair. His mom was carrying a glass of water from the kitchen, and she handed it to JD, who appeared nervous, uncomfortable. He'd done nothing to make any of this easy for her. He dumped his bag by the door, seeing JD's on the bench against the wall.

"So you probably all have a lot of questions," he started.

Danny was leaning against the wall and shot his hand straight in the air. "I have a ton only because I know way more, but since you told Mom and Dad you're married, are you going to share everything else?"

He stared over at Danny, who shrugged. He could see in his vibrant blue eyes that he wanted to kick his ass. *Okay, here we go.*

"Everything else… What exactly does that mean?" his mom said, appearing alarmed and sounding confused, and his dad now crossed his arms over his bare chest, tucking his hands under his armpits, looking from him to Danny, then over to his mom and JD. Evie was sitting quietly, watching, her long dark hair swept over her shoulders. She was wearing a mixed orange and brown shirt over blue jeans, but then, he'd never seen her dress any other way. JD was sipping on her water and staring into the glass as if she wanted to be anywhere but there.

Chris wiped his hand over his face, hearing the scrape of whiskers, trying to figure out what to say, where to start.

"Well, someone needs to say something," Jed said.

"Well, let's see," JD said suddenly. "My father had a shotgun, and his deputy, Ray, wanted to marry me. They've wanted Chris gone since he rode across the county line, and when my father had the judge there yesterday and said there was going to be a wedding with either Chris or Ray, Chris volunteered to marry me. Isn't that the long and short of it? Oh yeah, and Ray caught us by the river, with me naked and Chris almost, because we were about to have sex, and he arrested him on trumped-up charges in a show of force, I think it was…so now here we are."

Chris wasn't sure how to describe the shock on his mother's face and how his dad stilled. He wondered for a moment whether he had stopped breathing. Danny said nothing, but Mark was looking at him as if he were the coolest ever, likely because of the uncensored image JD had just laid out for everyone. He realized as he took in JD sitting there on the sofa, holding that glass, that she seemed very much alone.

"I don't even know where to begin," his mom said, "so I'm just going to say it. Have you lost your mind?"

Chapter Twenty-One

C hris's mother was nice, beautiful in a way that came from deep inside her, JD thought. She hadn't figured out his father, but there was something about him that seemed a lot like Chris, and she wasn't sure how they'd react as they listened to Chris finally give them a little more of what had happened from the minute he'd hit the county line. She could hear him talking but had stopped listening to what he was saying.

Her bag was resting on a bench beside the door, and she wondered whether that was where it would stay. It was only natural, she had to remind herself, to feel as if his parents wouldn't welcome her. After all, she didn't know them, even though they didn't seem like bad people. Awkward didn't even begin to describe the energy in the room. Everyone was quiet and seemed to be thinking some pretty heavy thoughts.

"So your family owns a lodge in Martin," Diana said.

It took JD a moment to realize that the way Chris's mother was talking and looking over to her wasn't filled with anything but curiosity, as if she didn't see JD as an evildoer.

She nodded. Her throat was dry even though she held that glass of water as if it were everything. Diana was now sitting beside her, and she actually smiled and reached over and patted her shoulder. She wasn't sure what Jed was thinking as he watched them both. His eyes were a shade of deep amber, but they had the same intense expression Chris's often did. She could see he got the blueness of his eyes from his mom, along with his red hair, but in everything else she was beginning to piece together, he took after his dad.

"Well, this is… I don't know what to say right now, because it's late," Diana said, "but you're home now, and, JD, you have to be exhausted, being on the back of the bike with Chris since early this morning. I'm pretty sure everyone has a lot of questions, but let's all get some sleep. We'll talk in the morning. Chris, you remember where your room is, I'm sure, so you get JD settled and show her where everything is, and turn off the lights in here when you go to bed." She actually stood, walked over to Chris, and reached up to pat him on the cheek. "Oh, how I missed you," she said.

Chris gave his mom an odd smile as she shook her head, walked over to Jed, reached for his hand, and pulled him down the hall.

"Well, I guess we'll talk in the morning," Danny said, then gestured to Evie, his wife, who had said nothing to JD. She had no idea what to make of her.

"Goodnight, JD. Nice to meet you," Evie said. Then she said something to Chris that JD couldn't make out. She didn't miss the smile, the soft laugh, the ease as Danny shoved a fist in Chris's arm before walking out the door.

Mark, too, started down the hall, shouting "Good-night!" behind him.

That left Chris and JD. The awkwardness between them had ramped up.

Chris pulled his hand over his neck and searched her out, letting out a sigh. "My mom's right," he said. "Let's go to bed. It's been a long day." He grabbed both their bags and took a step into the dining room, glancing back to her. "Come on, JD."

She made herself follow him to the rooms at the back, past a family room with a fireplace, a flat-screen TV, and a floral couch.

"Welcome to my room," he said, flicking on the light to reveal a masculine bedroom with pictures of motorcycles, horses, and family hanging on the walls. He dumped their bags on the floor by the bifold closet, and she just watched him, taking in the dark wood dresser, the neatly made double bed with its quilt of autumn colors. "Bathroom is out here," he said, gesturing to a room with a walk-in shower, separate bathtub, and double sink.

She couldn't help feeling as if she were a guest and nothing more. Even as he smiled, she felt awkward. "So why did you bring me?" she asked, and she couldn't believe she had, but at the same time she was glad, because she didn't like feeling as if she wasn't wanted, and right now that was exactly how he was making her feel. She wanted to weep for a moment over what she'd allowed to happen.

"What kind of question is that?" he said. He seemed mad and tired.

"A valid one, I think, considering how welcome I seem to be right now, or that's how I feel. I mean, I can't seem to shake this feeling that something has changed, the distance that's happening between us. I don't know how I fit. I wonder if maybe you're starting to think it would've been better to leave without me."

Her chest ached as the emotion she hadn't realized she'd been holding back started to build. She couldn't remember ever having felt so alone, and she was tired and sore from sitting on that damn motorcycle for so long.

Then he touched her, his hands over her arms, and when she looked up to him, she could tell he was angry. The way he held her so tight, she thought he might shake her.

"You know what this is?" he said. "Tiredness. I'm exhausted and relieved to be home. There's nothing more, JD, so stop trying to read something into nothing. I want to go to bed, that's all. Can we please just go to bed, get some sleep?"

He lifted his hands to her cheeks, holding her. Then he pressed his lips to hers, kissing her deeply. When he pulled away, she didn't know what to make of him. He stepped over to the shower and flicked it on, then shrugged out of his leather jacket, pulled off his T-shirt, and unfastened the bike leathers he wore over his blue jeans.

He looked up and over to her as he peeled off his clothes, the steam pouring from the shower, filling the room. Then he was naked and walking over to her, resting his hands on her shoulders and skimming them under her jean jacket. He slipped it off onto the floor with the pile of his clothes, unexpected but not unwanted.

"Come on, get undressed. Let's shower. I don't want to talk anymore," he said, then lifted her shirt over her head.

She could feel the chill in the air and welcomed the warm water, which looked so inviting, so she unfastened her bra and watched as Chris walked into the glass shower, under the spray. JD stepped out of her jeans and dumped her bra, socks, and underwear with them in a pile on the floor, then followed him into the shower and pulled the glass door closed.

Chris gave her all his attention, reaching for the soap as she stepped under the spray. After soaping up and scrubbing shampoo over his head, he pulled JD to him and started running the soap along her body.

It was so intimate, feeling the roughness of his large hands as they ran over her skin, her stomach and her breasts. If she shut her eyes, it was so confusing, because she could feel from his touch that he cared. She leaned back against him for a moment before he moved her so they were both under the spray, pulling her with him, rinsing off the soap as the warm water poured over them. Then he lowered his head and kissed her, pulling her to him, his hands sliding down her body.

He pressing her back to the tiled wall as he lifted her, her legs around him, and he filled her deeply. His hands were on her ass, holding her as he moved in. It was hot and deliberate and slow, and she hadn't expect this, not tonight, but then he was kissing her and moving faster. She was lost in feeling him in her, around her, taking her. She felt handled, possessed, wanted by him, and for a moment she'd have sworn she belonged to him.

She was holding on to him, resting her hands on his shoulders as he pulled out again, pressing her flat against the tile wall and pounding into her over and over. "Chris…" she started, trying to be quiet, but she felt herself coming apart around him as he filled her with his warmth again and again. As the warm water poured over them, her heart pounded and she fought for breath.

He was still inside her as he kissed her cheek, her nose, her lips. Then he turned off the water, holding her to him. He pulled out and let her slide all the way down him, his one hand holding her, and reality hit.

"Ah, Chris, did you forget something?" she asked.

He stepped out and reached for a deep red bath towel, and she held her arms up over her breasts. He handed the towel to her as he reached for a second one, and she wrapped the towel around herself, but not before he could give her breasts another appreciative look. He ran the towel over himself, over his hair and his face, and then he stared at her as if he didn't have a clue what she was talking about.

"A condom," she said. "I kind of think you forgot one. As much as I enjoyed that…" She let the words fall away, and she saw from the expression on his face, as he pulled the towel away, the moment he realized exactly what she was saying—exactly what he'd done.

She wondered whether he'd say anything to her. He'd reacted instead of thinking of the consequences of his actions, and once again, she couldn't help feeling very much alone.

The sun was up when Chris woke, feeling JD wrapped around him. Her head was on his chest, her legs intertwined with his, and he could hear the familiar sounds of the ranch from his open bedroom window, the horses and voices that drifted from somewhere outside.

He really looked at JD. Her hair was a tousled mess, and she was breathing softly. Something about her had him repeatedly doing stupid things, as if he'd lost his ability to reason. Not only was he married now, but he could've gotten her pregnant the night before. Being a husband and father had never been on the list of things he wanted to do at this time of his life, but here he was, and he still had so much he wanted to figure out.

He eased his arm from under her and slid out of bed, doing his best not to wake her. She murmured something, and he stepped away quietly as she snuggled in. He knew she had to be exhausted, and although he was too, he was also one to never sleep in, awake with the sun no matter how late he stayed up.

He opened a drawer of clothes he'd left behind and pulled on a clean pair of jeans and socks, then dug out a Lakers T-shirt, one he hadn't seen in months. He stepped out of his bedroom and pulled the door closed behind him, then strode across the hardwood floor and into the family room.

"There you are," Diana said. "Was wondering how late you'd sleep." She was holding a coffee behind her desk in the glassed-in home office just off the family room, and she pulled off the reading glasses she now wore.

Chris stepped in and took in how bright it was, how familiar, yet how different it seemed because of how long he'd been gone. "What time is it?" he asked, taking in his mom and her expression as she lifted her mug and took a swallow.

"After nine," she said.

"Sorry, I was…"

Diana put her coffee down and gestured to the chair across from her desk. "I know you had to be tired, driving all that way after everything. Is JD still asleep?"

He nodded. "Yeah, I didn't want to wake her."

He didn't know what his mom was thinking as her familiar blue eyes met his from across the desk. "You know what? I have to say, Christopher, that you surprised me last night. Your dad and I talked a bit this morning, and I know he wants to have a word with you, but so do I. You do realize that the situation was kind of unusual and likely not at all legal, so if you're looking for an annulment, it would be pretty easy to get."

He hadn't expected that from his mom, and he crossed his arms over his chest. "I'm not looking for an out or for my marriage with JD to end. I made a choice, Mom, and although the situation wasn't ideal, it is what it is."

As soon as he said it, his mom rolled her eyes. His dad had once told him to fully explain anything he needed to justify, but the problem was that he couldn't justify this. He was now out of South Dakota and away from JD's father's clutches, and it felt as if the albatross around his neck had been wrenched away.

"Chris, I know you better than anyone and also know that you hold a lot of your father's ideals and values, especially not going back on your word. It's admirable and a damn good quality, but marriage is an important step and should be taken only by two who are truly in love. Going into it for any other reason is just asking for trouble, and yours, how it happened, is all of that. That's all I'm going to say on the matter. Think about it carefully, and then you and JD should sit down and figure out some things."

He took in his mom and the hard gaze that said she'd put a lot of thought into the matter, and then she lifted her hand.

"I'm not telling you what to do," she said. "I wouldn't do that. This is now between you and that girl in there, and if this is what you want, to stay married to JD, then of course we'll support you." She was leaning back now in her chair, and a smile touched her lips.

He hadn't said a word. He'd expected something, but with his mom, he was never sure what that would be. "Great. I take it there's coffee..." He gestured to the kitchen, standing up and moving to the door.

"Always. Oh, and your dad's outside. You should go have that talk with him now," Diana said, slipping her glasses back on, ready to get back to whatever legal case she was working on.

Chris made his way out of the office and stopped in the kitchen, seeing the half-brewed pot. He grabbed one of the teal mugs his mom loved and then spotted a plate of muffins, so he grabbed one and took a bite as he made his way to the door, where he opened the closet and spotted a pair of his old sneakers. He shoved the last of the muffin into his mouth as he sat on the bench to pull them on before starting to the barn, where he could see his dad walking two horses out into the corral.

"Well, about time you got up," Danny said. Chris didn't see him until he came out of the barn, yet his Bronco was gone.

"Where's Evie?" he asked, less out of curiosity than to keep the spotlight from immediately shining down on him.

"Visiting her parents. So JD's still asleep?" Danny said. His hair, Chris realized, was longer than he usually kept it, covering his ears. He was dressed in blue jeans and a button-up shirt smudged with dirt. So his dad had already put him to work.

"Yeah, she's tired, so I didn't want to wake her," Chris said, looking to the corral. His dad had spotted him and was approaching, wearing the same ratty cowboy hat he'd always worn since Chris was a boy, along with worn jeans, cowboy boots, and a long-sleeve western shirt. He was really digging into each step. There was nothing subtle about what he wanted. "So Dad wants to talk to me, Mom said."

Danny just shook his head. "Oh, I'm sure he has a few things to say to you. So do I, from 'What the hell were you thinking with?' to 'Seriously, dude, marriage?' Yeah, I can see she's gorgeous, beautiful, but is she who you want to be married to? A woman you've known for hours, a day?" Danny lifted his hands, maybe because of the expression on Chris's face.

"Great, you're up," Jed said, "because I want to have a

word with you about what you got yourself into." His dad took in Danny and then Chris.

Chris wasn't sure what he saw in his father's and brother's expressions, but he could tell they both wanted to have a go at him.

"And you," Jed said, turning to Danny. "I still can't believe you didn't tell us. You should have called us, considering your brother here got himself balls deep in a shitload of trouble. Seriously, Chris, what were you thinking? What were you doing?"

He could see how worked up his dad was getting, and he wasn't a man to get worked up.

"Answer me this," Jed said. "Did you go after the girl because of what her father did to you? Was all of this because you weren't going to have another man telling you what to do, how to feel or think?"

Chris's jaw slackened, and he knew he couldn't get away with not talking or explaining. "It wasn't like that, exactly," he said, except it was, and it had in fact started out that way. He saw the exchange between his dad and brother, their reaction.

"Then explain exactly what it is," his dad said. Even Danny was shaking his head as if he'd really screwed the pooch this time.

"Okay, so yeah, I was pissed off with her dad and the deputy for pulling me over for no valid reason and creating that bad cop, bad cop scenario. I had dinner with her, took her out, and the more they tried to push me away, the more I dug my heels in. If it had been anyone else but JD, I would've been gone. I never expected to meet this sweet, amazing woman who I wanted to get to know—and no, I wasn't ready to go, and I sure as hell wasn't about to let her dad run me out of town or threaten me like he did. Then there was her first husband and how that went to shit because of them."

He took in their faces. He'd just opened another door he hadn't planned on, and it had to sound even worse now. His dad shook his head, speechless.

"Look," Chris said. "Yes, she was married before at seventeen, but once her dad found out, he and his deputy dug up everything on her husband's background and found something they could use to make him go away, sign papers to get the marriage annulled as if it never happened. That was why I called you, Danny, after that cop was in my room that night, going through my things to dig up everything he could on me. I know, Dad, from the way you're looking at me right now, that you're still thinking I've lost my mind, but telling you is different than what it was really like. I made a decision, and yes, her father pushed and backed me into a wall, but at the same time, I remembered what they did to her ex. If JD ever knew the real reason he left—"

"I don't understand how you know anything about Matt."

Chris hadn't heard her come out. He turned around, taking in the hurt and something else in her expression. Her hair was pulled up in a messy twist, and she was wearing a simple blue sundress, her feet in flip flops, holding a coffee. The look in her eyes made him feel as if he'd betrayed her.

"Who's Matt, again?" Danny asked quietly, leaning closer.

Chris tossed him a glance over his shoulder but wasn't about to answer him. He needed to figure out how much she'd heard, though her expression said everything.

"My first husband, if you can call him that," JD said in

answer, looking right at Chris. "The marriage was annulled five minutes after my father found out, and I never saw Matt again. He up and left, but you say if I knew the real reason he left, I'd…what, go after him?"

Jed cleared his throat and rested his hand on Chris's shoulder. "Okay, you two need to talk about a lot of things, so we're going to leave you to do that. Clear the air and discuss whatever secret you're keeping. You two decide what you want to do. But a word of advice, Chris, and hear me on this: You have a tendency to dig yourself into a heap of trouble, and you need to realize your actions don't just affect you now. You have a wife," he added, his hand still on Chris's shoulder.

Then Jed gestured to JD, squeezing as if trying to drive his point home—as if he could ever have forgotten her. "Figure it out, talk it out, and do it with a cool head," he said, then stepped back and looked over to her. "JD, make sure you have some breakfast."

Chris shut his eyes. Even thinking about this, it didn't feel real. His dad and Danny were walking away into the barn, and he turned back to his girl, taking in the hurt in her face, the anger, the exhaustion, and sensing that things could turn sideways. He'd never meant to say what he had, and he wished he could go back thirty seconds and think before he tried to explain one more thing.

"Okay, listen," he said. "When we came back from the bar, Ray was in my room."

She was holding the coffee between both hands and looking at him, and he could see if he didn't hurry up, she'd likely slug him or something. Anger was anger in a woman.

"He'd gone through my things and went on to inform me of the details of Matt, who he was, and his past."

She shrugged. "What past? What are you talking about?"

This was one of those moments where he didn't like knowing something. This could hurt her, would hurt her. "He had a record. Did you know he'd spent time in jail?" he said. His coffee was cold, so he dumped it on the ground and stepped closer to JD, but she took a step back.

"No, I didn't…but there's more?" she said, making sure the distance stayed between them.

He nodded. "You sure you want to know?"

What was he doing? This wasn't the kind of thing he should share, but then, this was JD, and maybe he needed to know whether this would make the difference and have her walking away from him, looking for Matt, making a choice.

"Tell me," she said. Her expression seemed stilted, and he could see how tense she was.

"According to Ray, he wasn't going anywhere," Chris said, "and you knowing about his time in jail wouldn't have been enough to send him on his way—but what happened to him in jail was…" He couldn't say it, didn't want to say it. From the expression on her face, he wasn't sure she understood. "It's not the kind of thing any man wants anyone to know. Rape is different for a guy."

She stepped back, a look of horror on her face, and dumped her coffee.

"Hey…" He reached for her mug and took it, gripping her arm, but she yanked it away, pulling back again.

"Stop, just stop!" she said. "Are you telling me they blackmailed him because of what happened to him in jail, and because of that, because he didn't want me to know, he signed the annulment and left town? That was the reason?"

She was getting loud, and he could see his mom pop

her head out of the house. He half expected to see Mark, too, but he wasn't anywhere around.

"Answer me this, JD," he said. "Now that you know, does it make a difference? Would you go after him?"

He couldn't believe he'd asked, but when she didn't reply right away, he realized just maybe he had his answer.

Chapter Twenty-Three

Her head was spinning, and she couldn't grasp everything Chris had just said. She knew only that he was walking away, striding right past her, into the house, and the screen door slapped closed.

How could he be angry with her? She was still trying to understand.

She turned to see Diana standing on the front deck, her mouth agape, likely in shock. JD didn't know what to do. Considering everything that had happened in a few short days, it seemed as if the rug had been yanked out from under her again and again. She lifted her hand and ran it over her hair because she couldn't think of what else to do.

She was exhausted, having woken up when Chris stepped out of the bedroom and pulled the door closed that morning. She could have lain there and tried to go back to sleep, but she'd slipped from bed and pulled on the first thing she pulled out of her bag. She had needed to settle a lot of things with him: their home, their families, their marriage, and what the hell were they to do? But now she was at a loss.

"Well, I don't know what to say," she said to Diana. She couldn't believe Chris had just walked away, so she started up the steps to the deck and paused, taking in his mother's vibrant blue eyes, the same as his.

"You should go and talk to him," was all Diana said to her. "But before you do, JD, just be clear on what you want with my son, if you want to be married or not. If you do, let me tell you, you need to make sure the lines of clear communication are drawn. Say what you feel, and don't hide your feelings from him. And no secrets, because they always have a way of coming out of the woodwork."

She wanted to say something to that but didn't know what, so she just nodded and pulled open the screen door, then stepped inside, hearing a rustle in the kitchen. She walked around the corner and spotted Chris putting their mugs in the dishwasher.

He stopped and looked up at her. Yeah, he was angry, irritated, and had come to his own conclusions about her and her feelings, and that made her furious.

"Why would you ask me if I'd go after Matt? Oh my God, it just makes total sense now how you kept bringing him up," she said. "After everything that happened between us, I married you. I'm here with you now. I don't understand why…"

He closed the dishwasher and rested his hand on the counter, making a sound of frustration. "You're still in love with him. Knowing the truth of why he left, I'd think it would make a difference."

Why was he looking at her as if she'd decided already? She hated that feeling. She hated this distance.

"I have no idea what would ever make you think that,"

she said. "You just told me something important about someone I was in love with. At the time, if I'd known, it wouldn't have made a difference to my feelings for him, but the fact that he didn't stand up to my father and Ray and instead cowered and gave in, leaving without a word, thinking me knowing would make a difference… No!" She stepped closer to Chris. "How could you think it would make a difference to me now after all these years? Were you under the impression I would suddenly up and leave, go and track him down, and, what, get back together with a man who couldn't be all I needed him to be? Are you trying to say that I would somehow toss away everything that's happened between us and discount it as meaningless?"

He still hadn't said anything, and it was this quiet stubbornness staring back at her that had her wanting to ball her fists and yell at him. It was infuriating. She fisted her hand and tapped his chest with it.

"Say something!" she said, standing right in front of him. "I'm not in love with Matt LaCroix. There's nothing left there, because the only feelings I have are for you, Chris. I don't have any room here for anyone else." She pressed her hand to her chest, taking in his blue eyes, the way he stilled, the way he was looking at her. She reached over to him again, and he took her hand and pulled her closer until she was in the circle of his arms.

"So no Matt?" he said.

She shook her head.

"And this you and me thing, you're in?"

She nodded, wondering what he was thinking. "If you still want me after dragging me all the way out here to another place, another state, a long way from home," she added shyly.

He lowered his head and pressed a kiss to her lips, tasting her, letting the kiss linger, before pulling back. Her hands went to his face, feeling the whiskers. He still hadn't shaved, and she craved touching him, being this close to him.

"You have to ask that, really?" he said as he pulled back further. "I think I'd rather show you how much I want you." Then he lifted her and started out of the kitchen.

"Chris, put me down! We need to talk about everything. There's so much we have to figure out about our future and everything, and jobs, and a house, and…"

But he didn't put her down. As the screen door slapped closed, she took in his mom and dad in the doorway. Chris was holding her against him, his hand on her ass, her arms around him. His dad simply pulled his mom back out the door and closed it behind them.

"Okay, that was so embarrassing." She pressed her forehead to his, and he kissed her cheek, her nose. She couldn't help the laugh that bubbled up, but he was just looking at her with those blue eyes, the way he had looked at her the very first time she'd set eyes on him.

"So, Josephine Denise Friessen," he said, and he lifted her legs, giving her a bit of a toss and carrying her, "we've got some time to figure all that out, but right now, the only thing I want to do is get to know my wife a whole lot better."

What's coming next in The Friessens, Unexpected Consequences

Don't miss the brand new return of The Friessens novel KEEP ME IN YOUR HEART. Don't miss this new

Friessen release March 31, 2021. Click here to order your copy available from all retailers.

And don't forget to leave a review of In the Charm

Are you on Goodreads? Add to your TBR list on GOODREADS HERE!

Unexpected Consequences

A Friessen Family bonus short story

Brothers Chris and Danny Friessen return in a short sweet novella about unexpected consequences in their young married lives.

Chris and JD are just coming to terms with the fact that they're married despite barely knowing each other, and JD is learning that her husband not only has a dominant alpha side but is also impatient. Can the chemistry between them be the glue that holds them together?

Meanwhile, Danny and Evie are stuck in big-city Seattle, and between law school, studying, and work, Evie can never find the right time to share a secret she knows would be more than Danny could handle.

But, as both couples soon learn, life's little surprises could end up being a greater gift than they expected.

A pink plus sign was staring back at JD from the cheap plastic stick, and it took her mind, her eyes, a minute to register what this could possibly mean.

It couldn't be right. It had to be a mistake, considering it had happened only one time, one stupid moment in which her husband—and she was still having to remind herself of the fact that she was now Mrs. Friessen—had forgotten to wear a condom.

What was she going to do? Motherhood was nothing she'd expected at this time in her life, but she'd also never expected to be married to a man she hardly knew. She was only now discovering that the chemistry that rocked between them was basically all they had in common.

There was a knock on the bathroom door, and the knob rattled.

"JD." Chris was on the other side, sounding impatient. That was another thing about the man that she hadn't expected and had chalked up to a quirk of his personality, but it was turning into something that could become an issue between them, that dominant side of him that seemed to want to know what was going on with her, invading her space so much that she couldn't breathe.

The door knob rattled again when she said nothing, still staring at the plastic stick. Then she tucked it back in its wrapper.

"Just a minute," she said, turning on the water and then flushing the toilet, wondering what to do with the stick. She spotted the empty garbage and grabbed a wad of toilet paper to wrap it in before dumping it, and then she washed her hands.

When she opened the door, Chris was waiting there— or, rather, he was looming, his expression questioning. He stood in blue jeans and a faded T-shirt, with handsome features. The three-day whiskers he frequently had gave his face that messy, hot, and sexy look, especially with his blue eyes, which seemed so deep and mysterious.

Then there was his incredible ripped body, which didn't give her a moment's rest when he had her in bed, under him, driving into her and making her feel loved, special, and his. It was the only aspect of their relationship that worked, and it worked well. Sex with Chris was amazing, better than amazing, and it was the reason she was in the predicament she was.

"What were you doing in there?"

Was he serious? She shrugged and stepped around him in her sock feet, her blue jeans feeling snug and her baggy blue T-shirt hanging loose to hide the tightness in her belly.

"Bathroom, you know," she said. She could feel him right on her heels, watching her as if he knew she was hiding something from him.

"You feeling all right? You were gone a long time."

She wanted to roll her shoulders as she strode into the dining room and the tiny boxy kitchen of his parents' house, listening to try to get a sense of who was there and to figure out what to say.

"Sorry, didn't think I was that long," she said. "So, I should start dinner before everyone starts coming in and wondering where it is."

There, perfect change of subject. She knew she'd spent a questionably long amount of time in there, the entire time of peeing on the stick and waiting for the results, then another chunk of time from the horror of realizing her worst fear had just come true. But it had been her time, which was something Chris didn't seem to understand, considering the first thing he'd done when he walked in the door was look for her, call for her, and seek her out.

She pulled open the fridge and lifted out the bowl of chicken pieces she'd soaked in brine overnight, then closed it to see Diana appear around the corner, glasses perched atop her head, wearing a casual gray track suit that showed off her amazing figure.

"JD, you know you don't have to cook every night," Diana said. "Well, I just have to say it, but at the same time, I'm so glad you have. I'm truly enjoying it, and frankly, we're just never going to let you leave. It's settled. You'll have to stay here forever. My son didn't exaggerate your culinary skills. You're spoiling us, all of us."

JD knew Diana was teasing, but just hearing how much she was appreciated really meant something.

Chris was leaning against the counter, taking up more than his fair share of room in the kitchen. There was limited counter space, and she'd have given anything for the workspace she'd once had in the commercial kitchen of her family's lodge, with its gas range, commercial convection ovens, and oversized fridge. Basically, she'd have loved a kitchen where she could have the freedom to do what she wanted to do.

Chris didn't move and was still watching her, his arms crossed, not even glancing his mom's way, as if he hadn't heard a word she said. "You were gone a long time, JD— and don't think I haven't noticed how off you've seemed lately."

She could feel her jaw tighten, and she took in the way his mom was now staring from him to her as if she'd just realized something else was going on.

The door clattered, and JD heard heavy footsteps, knowing the sound of the way Jed, Chris's dad, walked.

"What's going on?" she heard him ask before he appeared in her line of sight beside Diana.

JD was still holding the bowl of chicken. She looked away and rested it on the counter, feeling the center of attention. "Was just about to start dinner, just a simple seasoned chicken over potatoes, carrots, beets, and onions. About fifty minutes in the oven should do it. I'll throw together a salad with a simple vinaigrette, and we should be eating in about an hour. Oh, and I think I'll whip up a batch of biscuits to go along with it."

She had to stop for a second and pull in a breath, as she felt the heaviness hit her again just at the thought of food, the scent, the smell—one of the reasons she'd picked up a home pregnancy test to begin with.

"Now you're ignoring me," Chris said. "That's just great, JD. I'm starting to think you're trying to hide something." He just didn't let anything go, another one of his quirks that was starting to put her on edge. She'd never considered having to share every minute detail of what she was thinking or doing.

"I'm not ignoring you, Chris. I'm making dinner, is all. I'm sure everyone is hungry."

He was more focused than a hound dog on a scent, not to be distracted. It was almost annoying, especially since she didn't want to talk about it, not right now, considering she was still freaking out inside.

When she glanced up, she took in her husband and his parents, who were watching them as if they'd realized they may have walked in on something. By the way Jed exchanged a glance with Diana, she wondered whether they'd add something, or maybe they too would start questioning her as to what was going on.

"You're trying to change the subject," Chris said. "Dinner can wait. Everyone can wait."

It wasn't lost on her, the authoritative tone he seemed to be taking more and more with her, another quality she wasn't sure she much liked.

"So what's going on?" Mark said as he appeared. He had the same red hair as Chris, and she thought he'd grown an inch in the past week. "What's for dinner?"

She wondered whether he was about to squeeze his way into the kitchen as well. The room really was made for one. "Chicken is what's for dinner," she said, pulling open the cupboard door and searching for a casserole dish, "and I'm doing my best to get it on and in the oven."

Chris stepped over and rested his hand over her arm to stop her, then lifted the dish out from the second shelf and set it on the counter. He was so close to her, and she knew he wasn't going to be brushed off. It was in his eyes, his expression. As young as he was, he made her feel as if he could handle anything. But this? She wasn't ready to tell him, considering she still hadn't figured out how to wrap her own head around it.

"Fine, if you want to know," she said and stepped to the side, seeing his family standing just outside the alcove to the kitchen, behind him in this awkward confined space. "This isn't the way I imagined saying it, and I haven't even begun to figure out how to make sense of this, but now that you have me on the spot…" She shrugged, taking in the expressions staring back at her, the silence. Yes, she had everyone's attention. "So here it is: I think I'm pregnant."

She didn't have to look directly at Chris's parents to know that she'd shocked the hell out of everyone, and she could feel the tension of the moment ramp up in that second as she breathed in and out, waiting for someone to say something.

"Oh, well." Diana finally broke the silence, and Jed cleared his throat.

For a second, she thought Chris had stopped breathing from how still he was and how intently he stared at her. JD rested her hand on her hip for lack of an ability to figure out what to do in this awkward moment. Jed was running his hands roughly over his face, and she worried for a moment about what he'd say. She was feeling responsible, but at the same time, she knew it took two.

All Jed did was cock his head and stare over to his son, waiting for him to say or do something. Instead of Chris saying something to break the silence and shock, though, all he did was reach for her wrist and pull her out of the kitchen, past his parents and Mark, who had an odd look on his face, toward his bedroom at the back of the house.

"Chris, what are you doing?" she said as he pulled her inside his room and closed the door.

His hand rested high on the frame, and he gestured to her. "What?"

That was it. He lifted his other hand in the air, his mouth open as if he was trying to figure out what else to say. Yeah, shock was an understatement.

"Yeah, that's exactly how I felt just moments ago after peeing on a stick, but the difference is, Chris, that I'm the one pregnant, not you."

J D was making dinner, and Chris was at a loss for what to say. To make it worse, she was now mad at him for a situation she was just as responsible for—but then, she'd basically sucker punched him, leaving him feeling as if he'd been dragged behind his bike and covered in road rash.

Pregnant, good God!

He didn't even have his future figured out yet, and he was trying to get his head wrapped around the fact that his plans were now completely toast. Everything he'd planned out for his future had been dumped in the toilet. The moment he'd ridden into Martin, his fate had been sealed —not that he regretted JD. There was something about her sweetness, having all that warmth tucked against him every night, and the sex was a perk of marriage he'd shamelessly and unapologetically enjoyed at every opportunity.

On the other hand, he was quickly getting to the point where he couldn't keep lying to himself over the fact that he wasn't exactly ready for this commitment. He'd expected to travel after socking away more cash, to enjoy his freedom, becoming a minimalist and focusing on his future, doing what he loved, when he wanted to do, and eventually carving out a piece of something somewhere just for himself. Now his future seemed to be taking a direction he'd never planned, and all his control had been ripped out of his hands.

"So what are you doing?" Jed said.

Chris hadn't heard his dad approach as he settled on the sectional in the family room in front of the big-screen TV, which wasn't on. "Nothing, just sitting here, trying to…" He gestured to the noise and clatter coming from the kitchen, where JD, his wife—another fact he had to remind himself of every minute of the day—was making dinner for his family, for him.

Jed glanced once over his shoulder toward the kitchen, his arms crossed over his chest. "Trying to what? Got to say, you're screwing the pooch big time on this one, manhandling her and dragging her off. Shit, Chris!" His dad gave a rough laugh under his breath. "Yeah, your mom and I heard you yell. Half the county did. Did you accomplish anything with that temper tantrum? I noticed you're here brooding right now while she's cooking us dinner. You should talk to her."

The way his dad was looking at him, Chris wondered whether there was a lecture coming.

"I tried," he said, "but she walked out of the bedroom. Pretty sure she's angry with me over this mess that isn't—"

"Hey, cut it out." His dad stepped closer, gesturing toward him. "This isn't the time to start pointing fingers and playing the blame game, arguing and fighting. You got yourself into a situation. You're married, and now that girl in there, who, I might add, your mother and I rather like, considering we've never eaten this well, ever… She's spoiling us," his dad added for effect. "Neither your mother nor I want to go back and start cooking. But JD's nice, and we like her a lot. We've noticed the fact that you can't keep your hands off her, so her being pregnant and having a baby on the way is a fact that you'd better get your head around right quick. Whether you like it or not, you're going to be a father, and either you get real about it right now or things are going to get worse for you."

So there it was: His dad was taking sides. He just stared up at Jed, who then reached down and smacked one of the legs Chris had crossed and rested on the coffee table, knocking them to the floor.

"Seriously, Chris, that's it? Grow up, now! I hate to tell you this, but you're going to need to start changing up how you handle things. You're going to have to be a grownup here. You chose to marry her, you. You brought her here. She's family now."

His dad sank down on the other end of the sectional.

"Hey, I just had the rug yanked out from under me," Chris said. "Shit, I thought something was up, but I didn't think it was this. I didn't think in a million years it would be this…"

He stared at the wall that separated the family room from the kitchen and the rest of the house, knowing JD was just on the other side. He leaned his head back and shut his eyes, groaning. When he looked over to his father, who was sitting there, watching him, he could see there was a hint of amusement in his eyes.

"So what am I supposed to say to her?" Chris asked. How was he supposed to pretend he was happy over something that was making him break out in a cold sweat? All he could see were dollar signs and his dreams of freedom crashing and burning, dreams he hadn't even realized he was still holding on to.

"How about you just go in there and give her a hand with dinner? That would be a pretty big start, and then just listen if you can't figure out what to say. But grabbing her and dragging her to your room? Not really a smart move, Chris. And another thing, in case you missed it: She said she thought she was pregnant, as in she doesn't know for sure, so maybe you could also get your wife to a doctor and find out before you start freaking out. If she is, you and her need to sit down and get real on the fact that you're going to be parents, and you a father. You know that scared shitless feeling you have inside you right now? Well, hate to tell you this, but when you're a father, it never goes away."

For a second, Chris thought his dad was joking, but Jed didn't smile. In fact, his gaze took on an intensity and seriousness that packed a punch. Chris was feeling the discomfort of it as if someone had taken a fist, grabbed hold of his insides, and squeezed.

"A word of advice, Chris: A happy wife means a happy life. You want to be miserable, then you just keep on doing what you're doing, but you need to listen to her, talk to her, compromise." Then his dad stood up as Chris heard a vehicle.

"Danny and Evie are here," his mom called out.

"Go give your wife a hand in the kitchen" was all his dad said as he walked out of the room.

Chris didn't have a clue what to say as he started into the kitchen, hearing his dad outside now. He paused, taking in his mom, who was standing beside JD. Whatever they were saying to each other, they stopped, both staring at him as if they were discussing him and he'd interrupted them.

"Mom, if you don't mind..." He gestured, and his mom rested her hand over JD's shoulder and rubbed.

"Just remember what I said," Diana told her, then

stepped over to Chris and gave him a look that, while filled with love, let him know she was mad at him. She lifted her hand to his face as if memorizing every detail. All she said as she stepped out of the kitchen was "You need to shave," and then he listened to the door open and close.

That left just two.

JD kept doing what she was doing, making a salad and chopping up vegetables. There was a baking sheet on the stove top with biscuits cut and ready to go in the oven. She said nothing. So she wasn't going to make it easy.

He stepped closer to her and noticed the way she chopped celery with a lot more force the closer he got. "I'm sorry for the way I reacted," he said, and she stopped chopping and rested the knife on the cutting board. Her hand fisted and squeezed the handle. Then she turned and faced him, looking up at him, and he noticed she seemed pale and tired, or maybe he was reading too much into it.

He reached out and fingered a strand of her silky hair, and she shut her eyes at his touch, leaning into his hand. When he rested his hand on her shoulder, around her, she walked into his arms, kissed his chest, and slipped her own arms around his waist, snuggling against him.

"You're forgiven," she said in her sassy way that always made him smile. He pressed a kiss to the top of her head, holding her against him, feeling her breasts and all her softness.

"So, a baby. You think you're pregnant, but not for sure?"

She pulled away, stepped back, and he could see she'd taken it the wrong way.

"Now, don't go getting upset again with me," he said. "I just asked…"

She sighed and ran her hand over her head. "Home

pregnancy test, not doctor confirmed, but the tests are pretty much ninety-nine percent accurate."

He wasn't sure what she was thinking. Was she happy, sad, or what? And what should he say?

"So it's more than likely," he said, wishing she was wrong. Maybe she was wrong.

She shrugged. "Chris, I guarantee you I never expected that I would be married and living a state away from my parents at this time in my life, and now pregnant, when you and I are still trying to master the basics of just getting to know each other, all while living under your parents' roof. I don't have a clue what our future is. You're working for your dad here, and I'm just hanging around and cooking for lack of anything else. Then what?"

He rested his hand on her shoulder and tried to imagine what she'd look like carrying his kid. "We'll figure it out…" he said, then heard voices and footsteps. It sounded as if everyone was coming inside. He didn't look back, as he could see how on edge she was. "Let's have dinner. I'll help with whatever here, and then tomorrow we'll figure some things out, get answers for sure, and then make a plan."

He wasn't sure if that appeased her, but she seemed to relax a bit even though he was far from relaxed now.

"Everything okay here?" Diana poked her head in the kitchen, and he could see Danny and Evie, his wife, lingering by the dining table with Jed and Mark, talking and laughing.

Chris glanced back to JD. "Yeah, everything's good," he said, but as he said it, the words fell flat, because everything about this was anything but good.

Chapter 3

D anny didn't know what to say. He could feel the stress of everything piling on him and pulling at him from what seemed like every direction. It was a stress that had been building, starting in the pit of his stomach and now pulling across his shoulders and waking him in the night.

He'd felt it for a while, the pressure, the demand, spiraling as if everything was closing in on him. Everything, his dreams and future career, was taking a turn to something dark and nasty that he hadn't planned. As of late, his passion for the law and the future he'd seen for himself had been twisted into something he imagined would cause one problem after another.

He could hear the shower running and realized he should go in there and join Evie, join his wife, wash her back, be with her, but the fact was he needed a minute to himself, away from everything. He needed another minute to breathe and get his head around the fact that his wife was also pregnant.

All this had happened at about the worst time in his

life, their lives, because he still needed to pass the bar and gather options for his future.

"You okay?"

He looked up to see Evie standing there wrapped in just a towel, the end tucked in between her breasts. Her hair was pinned up on the top of her head, and she looked incredibly sexy. She could read him like a book. He squeezed the back of the chair. He hadn't heard her come out.

"Yeah, yeah. Just kind of blown away by the news about Chris and JD. Wow, a baby on the way."

Just like them. He wondered what he saw in Evie's expression. She wasn't smiling, and she nodded and pulled her gaze from him as she made her way over to the bed and pulled open one of the dresser drawers to lift out a T-shirt, one of his older ones that had never left the ranch.

She dropped the towel and stood there naked, her back to him, and he took in how tiny she was, her perfect ass, her slender legs, and her curvy waist and back, but he stayed where he was as she pulled his shirt on. It draped to her thighs.

She unpinned her hair. It was deep chestnut now, but she'd added highlights a few weeks ago during a trip to the salon in Seattle a block from where they lived in their cramped studio, a place so small there was no room for a crib.

"I noticed at dinner that you didn't once mention the fact that I'm also pregnant, that we're going to have a baby," she said as she reached for a brush on the small dresser and ran it through her hair, brushing the length over her shoulder.

He could feel the tension building. What did she want him to say? "I was taken by surprise, and I'm pretty sure neither Chris nor JD expected Mark to blurt out that they have a baby on the way. Did you see how quiet they were, and they've known each other how long? Only a few days before they got married, and they've only been back here for…"

He took in the way Evie lowered the brush. Her glance was filled with even more annoyance.

"They've been here for four and a half weeks," she said, "and I'm not sure why you're so focused on them. That's your brother's business. How about a little more interest in us, me, and what we're going to do? Don't think I haven't picked up on how freaked out you are. I get it, considering you've said nothing about the baby, my pregnancy, and what all this means. So maybe ask yourself how that makes me feel." She wasn't just mad; she was hurt.

He ran his hands roughly over his face, hearing the scrape of his whiskers, and then he stepped away from the table and forced himself to move one foot in front of the other over to Evie until he was standing right in front of her. He rested his hand on her shoulder, feeling the soft cotton of his shirt.

"I'm sorry." Those were the only words he could think to say, as he was reeling still from her greeting just the day before when he'd walked into their apartment after a losing case in the public defender's office. The defendant hadn't stood a chance and was now stuck in prison for something he shouldn't have been. Danny had come home to his wife, who'd been standing there, waiting for him, looking tired and alone, and she'd hit him with just two words before he could take off his coat: "I'm pregnant."

It was just the timing, was all.

She lifted her chin and looked up at him, and he could see then the exhaustion and worry. It was even more pronounced, and at the same time, he could see how much she needed him.

"We'll tell everyone in the morning," he said, wondering how his parents would react, considering this hadn't been in the plan—not yet, anyway.

"And then what? You've been silent since I told you, and I can't help feeling as if you blame me in some way."

There it was, the elephant in the room. The fact was that he really did, even though he tried to tell himself he didn't, that it wasn't rational. They'd been careful, so how had it happened?

"I just didn't plan for this, not yet," he said. "I'm still months away from being done school, and I need to pass the bar and land a decent job that will pay to support you and a baby."

He thought about how Evie's check and tips from waiting tables paid for half their expenses in a place that wasn't cheap to live. No, it was beyond ridiculously expensive. At the same time, now he could feel how on edge she was, taking it all wrong, everything he was saying.

"But we'll figure it out," he said. "I'll figure it out."

She glanced to the side, to the stairs of the loft at his parents' ranch, a space that had been his, a refuge on weekends when they could get away, but for how much longer?

"And then what?" she said. "I know you've changed your focus and the direction of your career since we moved to Seattle and you started law school. At one time, you wanted to come back here and work with your mom, but over the last year, I've heard you talk more about staying and getting feelers out to some of the bigger firms, maybe even staying with the public defender's office. Is that still what you want? How are we going to afford it? We'll need a bigger place, too."

Did she have any idea what she was doing? Dampness

rolled down his back. She was voicing everything that worried him.

"I know all of that, Evie. Why do you think I've not been able to say anything? Because I don't know how to make all this work."

The moment he said it, he wanted to take it back, as her eyes widened and she stepped out of his arms.

"You don't know how to make this work? In what way, Danny? This baby is going to happen…or is that what you're hoping, for it not to happen?"

He couldn't believe she'd said that or could think it. "No! Now you're putting words in my mouth. I never said that."

"But you were thinking it, Danny. You seem to forget I've known you a long time, and I knew when I told you that you wouldn't take it well, but I couldn't put it off any longer, no matter what. As I watched you stressing about everything, the long hours you were putting into that last case, and studying, there's been less and less time for me."

He just stared at her, realizing what she'd said. "So how long have you known you're pregnant?"

She was standing just out of reach, and he didn't try to close the gap. He couldn't, as he stared at her, seeing this was worse than he'd thought. How far along was she?

"Evie?" he asked, and she stared straight at him.

"A while," she said, and he waited, his heartbeat kicking up as she crossed her arms over her breasts. "Almost six weeks."

S he ran her hand over the horse's mane, the dapple gray she rode every time she and Danny came home to the ranch, a place she loved, a place where she felt comfortable—only now she didn't know what to do, considering their lives were about to be changed forever.

"He misses you riding him, and he doesn't get out as much as he should."

She turned her head to see Jed, her father-in-law, striding toward her with sweat running down his brow as he pulled off his work gloves and brushed dust off his worn jeans. The sun was out, but she wanted to go back upstairs and lie down for another hour or two. She just wasn't feeling well this morning, as she hadn't for the last number of weeks.

He rested his forearms on the stall next to where she was standing. "So Danny filled us in this morning, another baby on the way. Two grandchildren." He was shaking his head, and for a minute she didn't know whether he was happy or sad. Then he gave her all his attention, and she wasn't sure what to think when an easy smile touched his lips.

"How're you feeling?" he asked.

She didn't know what to say, so she shrugged. "Tired, but okay."

So that was where Danny had gone, over to his parents' place. She'd woken with the sun streaming in the window and the spot next to her empty.

"You should go in and eat breakfast," Jed said. "JD has been spoiling us by doing all the cooking. She's left a plate for you."

She couldn't help but suspect there was a reason her father-in-law was here now instead of her husband. "So where is Danny?" she said.

"He and Diana are going over some things, some legal case. I've learned to stay out of the way and out of that business. He said you've known for a while about the baby but didn't tell him."

There it was, her secret. She was just past three months along and feeling every bit of it.

"Can you blame me, considering everything he has on his plate, with law school, studying, and working at the public defender's office? He comes home exhausted. I tried to tell him a few times, but the first time he fell asleep, and another he was distracted and focused on researching to prepare for a big case he was assisting on. Then there was Chris, his predicament and sudden marriage, so I just waited, telling myself I would say something after the case, when it calmed down. Then it became clear that was as calm as it would get. It wouldn't slow down, he wasn't going to relax, and I couldn't wait any longer, because I'd be showing soon, and then eventually he'd notice."

The horse nuzzled her, and she patted him again,

brushing back his forelock and rubbing his forehead. She glanced over to Jed and saw Diana striding from the house to the barn, wearing blue jeans and a simple T-shirt, her long red hair pulled up.

"Danny's a big boy, and he can handle more than you think," Jed said. "You should have told him, but I'm not here to tell you that. I can see you're worried, but you shouldn't be, because it won't fix anything. If you're waiting for a better time, it'll never happen. The best time to tell things is right away, not to wait." Jed turned at the sound of Diana approaching.

"Hey, there you are!" she said. "Danny said he thought you were still sleeping."

How could she sound so happy? Then, Diana always did, and she made Evie feel so good. Her hand skimmed over Jed's back as she strode past. They were so in love with each other still. It was something she'd always noticed about Danny's parents. Then her hand was around Evie, turning her so she was steered and walking in the direction of the house. "Danny told us the news this morning. It's so exciting, a baby, another one."

Why couldn't Danny sound as happy as his mom? Evie spotted Chris pulling on his helmet, straddling his bike, and starting it before JD got on back behind him. Then they pulled out and drove away.

Diana lifted her hand in a wave as they strode to the house, her arm still around Evie. "I wish he'd consider getting something safer now," she said. "Having JD on a bike isn't practical anymore or safe, not with a baby on the way. I think his father should have a talk with him."

Diana patted her shoulder, her arm still around her. Evie wanted to ask where they were off to, Chris and JD, as Diana led her up the steps inside the house and then sat her down at the kitchen table, where there was a glass of orange juice.

"JD made French toast and sliced up a platter of fruit," Diana said as she appeared with a plate and rested it in front of Evie. "I know Chris told us JD did all the cooking at her family's lodge, but I had no idea how good she is. It's like having our own private chef."

Diana placed butter, maple syrup, and a knife and fork in front of Evie as well as a plate of mixed fruit. Evie knew she should be hungry, starving, but the fact was that on mornings as of late, food was about the last thing she wanted. She touched the plate and went to push it away, but Diana pushed it right back as she sat.

"Yeah, I know that feeling, but you'll feel better with some food. Trust me, just try a bite and then another, even just some fruit, at least. You need the nutrition for the baby." She tapped the table.

"So where is Danny?" Evie said. She couldn't hear anything. The house was so quiet. She poured the syrup and picked up the knife and fork, staring at the thick bread cooked to perfection. Her mouth should've been watering.

"In my office, doing some research."

She cut a piece and then shoved it in her mouth and chewed. It was really good, and as she chewed and swallowed, Danny appeared, holding a mug and taking her in.

"You're up," he said, going into the kitchen and pouring a coffee. He seemed different this morning, not as tense, but then, every time they came home to the ranch, he seemed to decompress.

"I am. I'd love a coffee, too. Can you pour me one?" she asked as she dug into the French toast and sopped a piece in the syrup.

"You sure you should be drinking coffee now, being pregnant?" Danny was standing behind his mom, holding his coffee, and she just stared up at him. Who was this? He sounded calm, and now he was telling her what to do?

"One cup isn't going to hurt," Evie said.

Diana scooted back her chair. "She's right, Danny," she said. "Listen, I have work to do, and you two need to talk. Danny…"

The way she gestured to him, it wasn't lost on Evie that there was something more, as if they'd talked about something. When Diana was gone, Danny rested his coffee mug on the table, and she reached for it and took a swallow. She needed the caffeine pick-me-up and was damn sure going to enjoy it. Danny was still staring down at her, his hands resting on the back of the chair. His bold blue eyes were intense, and it seemed he had something on his mind.

"So what is it?" She gestured to him and pushed the plate away as she leaned back in the chair. Still holding his coffee, she took another swallow.

He tapped the chair with his fingers. "I've been thinking about your situation—our situation," he quickly corrected.

She said nothing and took another swallow.

"I think it would be best if we moved back here," he said.

She rested the mug on the table and couldn't have been more surprised. "You can't be serious. I know how hard you've worked, Danny. For a long while, you've been talking exactly the opposite. You love your work at the public defender's office, and you still have law school. I know you've been talking about what comes after, getting in with one of the bigger firms in Seattle, and now you want to come back? That makes no sense."

He was shaking his head and pulled out the chair where his mom had been sitting. He was so close to Evie, and he reached for her hand and pulled it over in between his. "Yes, I was, but I realized after a long night and the little bomb you dropped on me that we don't have that luxury anymore—and don't look at me like that," he added as she went to yank her hand away. He didn't let go and was staring at her with everything.

She had all of his attention. She couldn't remember the last time that had happened. "And how would you like me to act when it seems you're blaming me for being pregnant?"

"Evie, I'm not blaming you, and I'm sorry if it sounded like that. You're right, I was thrown when you told me, because this wasn't in the plan. But then last night, hearing about how long you were keeping it from me…when did we start doing that, hiding things, keeping secrets?"

Okay, now he sounded mad, and the way he said it made her feel for a minute as if she was wrong. She went to say something, and his rough hand was still holding hers, rubbing smooth circles. It was calming, and she realized it had been a while since they'd connected like this, with just a simple touch instead of the craziness of being busy, which was all they'd been for so long.

"So you want to move back here and do what?" she said.

This time he let go of her hand as he leaned back and rested his arm over the back of the empty chair beside him. "Doing what I should have all along, what I'd planned all along: starting a practice with my mom here in North Lakewood."

She wasn't sure she'd heard right, even though she knew that was what he'd wanted way back before they drove away from the ranch to Seattle, where he'd started law school. "And what about Seattle and everything you wanted there, the big firms, the public defender's office, school?"

He didn't shrug. He said nothing for a minute. She hoped he wanted this and wasn't settling. "I got real overnight about our life, our future, and being back here. It's where we should be, where we need to be. I'll finish school, and we'll move back before the baby, and here is where we'll settle. It'll be better. I want family around when you have the baby, yours and mine," he added.

She didn't know what to say. She hadn't expected this from him. "You'll be okay with this?" she said, but he didn't reply, and the way he tensed and looked around, she knew he wasn't. She stood up and took in the breakfast still on the table, half eaten. "No." She rested her hand on the back of the chair, putting distance between them.

"No to what?" He frowned, and she could see his disbelief and hear his frustration.

"No to all of it, Danny. As much as I want to be back here and would love nothing more than to have family around, what I don't want is for you to blame me. You doing this now, I'm afraid it will come between us. You'll blame me for your missed opportunity, your chance to be bigger, better. I don't ever want to be the reason you passed up on your dreams." She tapped the chair and gestured with her thumb to the door. "I'm going to go lie down."

Danny was still sitting with a furious and confused expression, and she knew he was at a loss for what to say, but what she also knew was that he didn't really believe everything he'd just told her, and that hurt more than anything.

"Evie," he called out to her as her hand rested on the door.

She turned back to him, glancing to where he touched her plate and looked over the room before his gaze landed on her.

"Sometimes we have to make sacrifices," he said, and it was exactly the wrong thing to say. Didn't he get that?

She nodded, a lump jamming in her throat. "You're right." She pressed open the door and kept walking, letting the screen shut behind her. She loved Danny, and she wasn't about to force him to pick between her, the baby, and his dreams.

"So it's official. JD is pregnant," Chris said as he strode into the barn ahead of her to find his dad stacking bales of hay for storage from a flatbed trailer outside.

JD was still reeling from all of it, including the fact that Chris had had the foresight to make a call to his mom's doctor and had gotten her right in that morning. Now, after a bunch of tests, a quick exam, prenatal vitamins, and a list of dos and don'ts, here she was, back at the ranch, with an expected due date of less than seven and a half months—the result of the one time Chris had forgotten to wear a condom. She wondered at what point she could point out to Chris that this unplanned pregnancy and baby mistake was all on him.

"That's great," Jed said. "I take it everything is okay and went well at the doctor's?"

Meanwhile, Danny was hefting a bale of hay, sweat staining the back of his light blue T-shirt. He dumped the bale and pulled off his worn old gloves before walking over. She wasn't sure what to make of his expression as he stared at her and then Chris. He nodded once.

She wondered whether the awkwardness was about her or his own predicament, which she'd overheard that morning. Evie was pregnant, and Danny was far from happy about it—or maybe it was her. She wondered whether he even liked her.

"Fine, fine," Chris answered for her, but his dad was watching her and then his son.

"JD, I know Diana will be happy to hear that, and she was thinking of doing something with you and Evie today…"

The door to the loft opened, and JD took in Evie, who had appeared. She was in blue jeans and an autumn-colored shirt, her hair hanging loose. JD didn't miss the tension that seemed to ripple between her and Danny. What was that about? This was the first time she'd seen Evie and Danny watch each other from a distance the way couples did when they were fighting.

No one said anything, but the way Jed looked from JD to Evie and then over to his sons said everything. "Okay, Chris, Danny, saddle up," he said. "We're going for a ride. Evie, JD, you two come with me." He tossed the work gloves he was holding onto a bale of hay as he walked over to Evie and then rested a hand on her shoulder.

"Yeah, Dad, I've got some things to do," Chris started. "JD and I…" He stopped, likely from the heavy gaze his dad leveled his way.

Jed gestured to Evie. "Come on, Evie," he said, then started over to JD. "Chris, you and JD can talk later, and whatever you need to do can wait. Saddle up. Come on, ladies."

Jed somehow had Evie and JD walking to the house, his hands resting on each of their shoulders as he walked between them, saying, "You two are needed by my wife."

He opened the door, and JD let Evie step in first before

she followed and took in Diana, who looked up from where she was at the table with a coffee and her glasses on, reading something.

"Here they are," Jed said. "I'm going to take those two numbskulls for a ride. Mark!" he called out.

JD didn't know where to look as she strode into the house.

"Mark's gone," Diana said. "He's at Roger's for the day, but you take your time. I have plans for us. We'll sit down, spend some time together."

Jed walked over to Diana and lingered a minute as he rubbed her shoulders and then kissed her. He said something JD couldn't make out, but whatever it was had a smile deepening on Diana's face. She radiated happiness. His hands, the way he touched her and she him, it was so intimate, and JD found herself exchanging a glance with Evie. It wasn't lost on her how little they knew about each other, this family she'd been living with for a matter of weeks. Then Jed was gone.

"Well, you two, this is exciting," Diana said. "Me and my two pregnant daughters-in-law, who'll give me some grandbabies I can spoil. I figured I would have some time with you two, kind of a girls' day, you know, and let Jed take your husbands out. Come on, let's go out back on the deck. It's a nice day, and I've made some lemonade. Sorry, JD, not fresh squeezed! I just don't have your magic touch."

Diana was in the kitchen, lifting a jug from the fridge and resting it on a tray. The table already held three glasses along with a plate of cheese and crackers and another with the leftover fruit from breakfast. "JD, grab the fruit," she said. "Evie, the plate of cheese and crackers."

They followed Diana to the back of the house and onto the deck, which overlooked a large tree with huge branches, a grassy area, and a fire pit with lawn chairs around it. The table had eight cushioned chairs as well as a barbecue they often used for grilling burgers and steaks any time they felt like a dinner out back. That was the only time JD wasn't behind the stove in the tiny kitchen.

"This is nice," Evie said as she sat in a cushioned chair, and JD noticed she pushed the plate of cheese and crackers far away from her as she made a face. Evidently, she was suffering.

"Yeah, it is," JD added for lack of anything better to say. She took in the expression on Diana's face as she looked from Evie to her.

"Oh, come on, you two," Diana said. "This is a happy time."

Was she kidding? It was anything but, because any thought she may have had before of her and Chris calling it quits and walking away from each other was now gone forever—not that she'd considered such a thing, but she'd realized that morning that the uncertainty of the future was what had been lingering in her mind.

"Well, I don't know about happy," JD said. "I think it's shocking, unexpected, and I'm feeling just how completely unprepared we are."

Evie widened her eyes and gestured with the flat of her hand across the table. "Exactly what JD said, but add in the blame game. Seriously, Danny acts as if I alone am responsible for this predicament, and now he has to play hero and squash his dreams, making me feel as if he's having to settle. It'll come between us eventually. Somewhere down the road, he'll resent me and the baby," she added.

JD just stared at Evie, wondering how she'd read her mind. "I couldn't have said it better," she added.

"Hmm, well, I can see how you would both take it that

way, considering the circumstances," Diana said, "but how about both of you listen to me? I for one couldn't be happier about the babies, and I look forward to being able to spoil them. There, I said it. Now, both of you likely didn't expect this, and you're both trying to get your heads around the fact that you have a baby growing inside you, my grandchildren. Well, let's be grownups here: Sex leads to babies. It happens, and once everyone gets past the shock…and yeah, I know that first minute when you find out, it's like 'Holy shit! I'm pregnant.' Then, having my sons respond like the unthinking males they can be, you didn't get the response you needed or wanted. You felt…" Diana was pouring lemonade and then paused, taking them both in.

"You mean the way he makes me feel as if it's all my fault?" Evie blurted out. JD stared right at her.

"Yeah," she agreed, "like I was the only one responsible for this, when it wasn't me who forgot." JD pressed her lips together, reminding herself this was Chris's mom, and a sex talk wasn't something she wanted to happen.

"Well, I've already seen how well you two have handled this, but my sons likely didn't respond how they should have. Hate to tell you both, but men often have a plan, and when things don't go accordingly, they say the first thing on their mind when what they need to do instead is dial it way back and listen first. I've been married a long time and love Jed deeply, but I'll tell you, there've been many times when I've wanted to yank my hair out because of something he's said or done. Men want to solve problems, but there're times problems can't be solved. They come at situations like they can be fixed, and they sometimes say and do things with zero tact. I remember what it was like, being pregnant. All your emotions are hyper, and you want sensitivity and support and understanding."

Diana slid a glass of lemonade over in front of JD and then Evie. JD reached for the glass, lifted it, and took a sip. Not bad. She wasn't sure where this pep talk was going.

"Evie, you and Danny have known each other since you were kids," Diana said. "You're the love of his life, and yes, I've noticed for a while the load Danny has taken on. He's stressed, but law school will do that, and so will the public defender's office. I did get the distinct impression this morning that he likely said everything all wrong, but he's right about one thing: You two need to move back here for now."

Evie was shaking her head. "Diana, he doesn't want to come back. He wants to crush the big city. He wants the challenge of a big firm and the complexity of those kinds of cases. If you'd have asked me this before we left for Seattle, before he started law school, I'd have said differently, but he's changed there. He'll regret leaving Seattle, leaving his opportunities. I've watched Danny over the last long while, and he's changed so much. He's dedicated, driven, and he'll blame me for having to give up his dreams."

Evie was so matter of fact, and JD just listened, because she didn't know anything about their issues. Chris never shared anything about his brother. That was the kind of thing women did.

"You're wrong, Evie," Diana said. "I know Danny, and while you do too, I understand that he may just be caught up in the big-city adrenaline rush. He thinks that's what he wants, but he'd be miserable. He likely doesn't even know it yet. Yes, he'd probably work a year or two with those big firms, but it's not uncommon to work eighty hours plus for weeks on end. He'd never see you and the baby, and your marriage would suffer, and he'd burn out. Danny would eventually make a decent income, and you'd raise the baby alone, and then what? Strangers living together away from your family."

JD couldn't imagine that kind of life. She'd been born and lived her whole life in a small town. She didn't know anything else and didn't want to know anything else. Her mother was there, her father was there, her grandparents, and now she was here. She still needed to call her family and let them know about the baby.

"And, JD," Diana said, turning that megawatt blue gaze on her. JD could see so much of Chris in her expression, an older, wiser Chris. "You and Chris are still at the stage of getting to know each other and figuring out what he wants to do. Guys don't often handle their life suddenly turned upside down well, especially as young as he is. At times it sounds as if he's blaming you, but in truth, he's just reacting."

Diana leveled her finger between them. "So you two need to sit them down, both of them, and tell them what you need. I guarantee you they'll get their heads in the game. They will come around, and in a few months, you both are going to have those beautiful babies, and I guarantee you that the panic you've seen in Chris and Danny will change to them doing everything for you and their kids, suddenly knowing what's really important: family. This here now, how you're feeling as if nothing will work out and this isn't what you planned, will suddenly go away the moment you hold your baby."

JD reached for a piece of cheese and cracker and took a bite. "And what about me and Chris? I mean, we can't live here forever."

Evie gave her a pointed look and also nodded. "Me and Danny too. Every weekend or thereabouts we come back to the loft, and I love it, but..." Evie really understood what JD was saying and thinking.

"Oh, I see," Diana said. "We're still at that stage, are we? Well, let me set your minds at ease. This is a big property, and for now, this is home. I mean, JD, if you and Chris had stayed in Martin, where would you have lived?"

Well, of course they'd have lived with her parents at the family lodge, but then they'd been tossed into something neither of them was ready for or wanted, right? She didn't say anything for a second.

"Okay, point taken," she admitted, "but—"

Diana shook her head. "No buts. We're family. Evie, the loft is yours and Danny's for as long as you want it, of course. This isn't the time to be off finding a place. No, you stay here for now. This is home. The fact is that young people today can't afford their own places, and I know Jed was planning on talking with the boys about this anyways. All of this will be theirs one day."

"So you want us all to stay here, live here?" JD said. She hadn't expected this and wasn't sure how it would work.

Diana nodded. "I do."

"And what makes you think Danny is going to come around?" Evie blurted out from where she'd been sitting rather quietly. Then she reached for cheese and crackers. Evidently she was hungry now and didn't look as pale.

"Because Danny loves you and his family, and when he comes back here, that passion and fire he had for the law and the reason he got into it is going to come back. Trust me on this, Evie. Lawyers are needed everywhere. Here it's just a slower pace, but he can do the kind of law he'll want. So, both of you, sit your guys down tonight and tell them what it is you're feeling. More importantly, you both need to tell Danny and Chris what it is you need, because I guarantee you their response will likely surprise you."

JD glanced across the table to Evie, whose expression

seemed much like hers. "And if you're wrong?" she asked and swallowed, because she didn't think Diana was really seeing Chris for who he was. Or maybe it was her.

A slow, easy smile lifted Diana's lips, and she rested her elbow on the table and her chin on her hand, taking in Evie and then her. "You seem to forget I'm married to their father, and our sons are very much the kind of men we raised them to be. They may be difficult, saying everything wrong, but deep down, you and those babies are and will be the most important things in their lives."

Chapter 6

"I've got two more groups booked in before the snow falls this year," Jed said. "They're sizeable, three days out. I'm thinking of surprising your mother and taking her down to Cancun for a few weeks, so you can hold the fort down and run things here."

Chris's dad looked over to him from his quarter horse, wearing his ratty cowboy hat and sunglasses. Chris had opted for a ballcap, since cowboy hats had never been his thing. He'd ridden the Arabian, one from the herd, only a handful of times. Danny, though, trailed behind on the Morgan, his horse, which he'd trained and ridden every weekend he was at the ranch.

"Fine," Chris said, seeing his dad was leading them to another trail further up the meadow, the opposite way to home. At this rate, it would be another two hours before they made it back.

"And Mark will stay so you and your brother can keep an eye on him," Jed said and glanced back to Danny, who was unusually quiet, especially considering he never had a shortage of things to say.

"You seem to forget we live in Seattle," Danny finally said, and Chris noted his response was quite sharp.

His dad shook his head. The way his face lit up, anyone could've been fooled into thinking he was happy, but they'd have been wrong. "You seem to have forgotten a lot of things, Danny," Jed said.

He whipped his horse around, forcing Danny to pull up, and so did Chris. The horse sidestepped, but the way his dad rode, he was one with that horse. It was second nature, as if they were of the same mind.

"The fact is," Jed began, "you promised to love that girl, and marriage and babies come with that. The way you're acting, it's as if she's the one who pulled the rug out from under you, but I hate to tell you, it was you who was entirely responsible. The timing may not be what you like, both of you..." Jed took in Chris, pulling him into this conversation. "It is what it is. Babies rarely happen when you plan them, and if you're waiting for the perfect time, well, they would never be born.

"Both of you need to pull your heads out of your asses and consider for a minute how JD and Evie are feeling. In case you've forgotten, they're the ones carrying your babies. They're the ones who not only have your children growing inside them but also can't just take a minute and walk away from the situation, because it's there with them. What do you say when the woman you love tells you she's pregnant? Let me give you a hint, considering you both blew it. It isn't the first thing or even the second thing you're thinking. You don't bring up all that panic and freak out over how you're going to afford this, your finances, your dreams, your future, your freedom..." Again, he was looking at Chris. "That's exactly what you don't say or talk about. You need to have more tact, more understanding than you've ever had, and just listen to her, her needs, her wants, because she's the one having her life, her body turned upside down. You both got that?"

What was he supposed to say to that? "I barely know her," he replied. He couldn't believe he'd just said that, because he loved having her around, in bed, touching her, kissing her, and he didn't think he'd be able to live without her if she left. He hadn't even allowed himself to consider everything.

"Yet you married her," Jed said. "Yet you brought her here, yet you got her pregnant. Shall I go on? Don't forget, your mother and I have seen you with her. If the next words out of your mouth are that you don't know how you feel about her, then that will be the first lie you've ever spoken."

Oh, geez, he couldn't remember his dad ever calling him out like this.

"And you," Jed said to Danny. "You came in this morning without Evie, ranting about her pregnancy and how it was going to ruin your life—*your* life—and how the timing was the absolute worst, about how you weren't going to be able to afford it, living where you're living and being so close to finishing school, writing the bar, and how you still needed Evie's check to pay the bills and couldn't have a crying baby in the house. Yet you sat down and talked to your mom about joining her and practicing law. Isn't that why you went to law school to begin with?"

Chris just stared over to Danny, seeing how irritated he was. Boy, their dad was really pulling out all the stops today.

Danny glanced away. "Look, I lost a big case, and someone who didn't deserve it lost his freedom. I've never expected to feel like this. It was just the timing. I sat Evie down and told her we were moving back here, but she said no. I'm willing to make the sacrifice, move back here, and then write the bar and set up practice from here, but she put her foot down and wouldn't hear it. She's being unreasonable."

That was the first time Chris had heard Danny speak about Evie like this. They'd always had a special bond, and even he didn't miss how it sounded.

This time, his dad did laugh. "You didn't tell her you're making a sacrifice, did you?"

Danny's expression said it all.

Jed glanced back to Chris. "Okay, listen up, you two. In case you didn't hear me the first time I said it, this isn't about you right now, or your feelings, or what works best for you, or in any way hinting that somehow the timing of the baby is messing up your plans. I can see why Evie said no. Seriously, Danny, is your career really more important than Evie, than the baby? What if she loses the baby, would you be relieved?"

His dad sounded mad, and Chris was glad the focus was on Danny. At the same time, his dad's words hit home. Yes, he wanted to travel, see the world, explore, but at the same time, if JD left tomorrow and there was suddenly no baby, he wouldn't feel happy or relieved. The thought actually saddened him.

His dad was looking right at him. "So here it is: Both of you sit your ladies down tonight and ask them how they're doing, what they're thinking and feeling, and make a plan without rehashing how it happened, because it doesn't matter how. Your wives are pregnant, they're carrying our grandchildren, and the only thing that matters now is that everyone is happy and healthy. Danny, you wanted to come back here and practice law, so do it now. You can always change up down the road after the baby, after you have things settled, if you decide this isn't what you really want.

"Chris, you've always had this wild free spirit, wanting to see the world and go it alone, but you have a wife now, and your single days of taking off and traveling alone are gone. Get your head around that. You can take over the business here for me and run it." His dad then turned his horse, who stepped over closer to him. "And if you too figure out down the road that this isn't what you want, then you can change it. Any questions?"

Chris wondered if the lecture was done.

His dad started walking his horse, but then turned to him again. "Oh, and in case you didn't realize it, your mom and I are thrilled that we're going to be grandparents."

Then his dad kicked up his horse and started up the trail. Chris looked over to his brother, who was just watching their dad. Neither knew what to say, feeling as if they'd just had their dad's foot planted in their backsides.

"Well, in case I didn't say it, congrats to you and Evie on the baby," Chris said.

This time, the hint of a smile touched the edges of Danny's lips as he glanced over to Chris. "Same to you, little brother."

Chapter 7

E vie heard the door softly close and the steps creak from the weight of his footsteps quietly coming up the stairs. Her eyes were closed where she lay resting on the bed. She couldn't remember ever feeling so exhausted before. She wondered if this was how she'd feel her entire pregnancy. She hoped not. It would really make it unbearable, and she'd get nothing done, and then there was work and waiting tables. How was she going to keep going?

She felt him standing there beside the bed, looking down on her.

She opened her eyes, looking up at him, with his red hair that needed a haircut and his blue eyes, which seemed different than they had been that morning. What had changed? She saw awe. His ego…maybe that was it. It was gone.

"Thought you were asleep," he said.

She was on her side and lifted her hand to her forehead, letting the back of it rest there. "Was just resting. I'm tired," she said.

Danny seemed to really study her, gazing at every inch

of her in a way he hadn't in a long time. Then he sat at the edge of the bed, right next to her, and rested his hand on her lower back and just touched her. "How're you feeling?"

It took her a second to understand what he was asking, to get past the accusation or something that continued to make her feel guilty. It wasn't there. It wasn't in his voice anymore.

"Good," she said, "just tired."

Actually, she was plagued with a constant nausea that seemed to be there from the moment she woke until she went to bed.

"Really?" he said. Again, he was sounding reasonable, and she wanted to ask what was up. It had to be a trick.

"Okay, I feel weak, nauseous, and so tired all the time. The smell of just about everything makes me nauseous."

Danny didn't look away, and his hand was now resting on her hip. She missed his touch, the simplicity of just being together, this closeness that had disappeared how long ago? She couldn't remember, as he'd become busy and they'd passed each other, her going to work, him coming home to study.

"I know I didn't handle this well," he said. "I'm afraid it's more because of the case I lost. I didn't realize the stress I carried, being so busy, but I really want us back here for now."

She didn't answer him, but there was something about the way he was saying it now that seemed so honest. "But it isn't really what you want," she said and waited for him to say again how nothing was going his way and what a mess this was.

"What I really want is for you to be happy, for our baby to be okay. Honestly, Evie, we don't have to say it's forever, kind of like when we went to Seattle. It wasn't supposed to be the forever place. Would you be okay for now if we came back here, if we had the baby here? We can decide down the road if this will be where I set up practice or maybe somewhere else, but for now, I really do want to move back here."

Was he just saying that? "I do want to come back here," she said. "Honestly, I don't know how much longer I can waitress. The smells are becoming too much, but I don't want to be the reason you give up your dream," she added, letting him take her hand and seeing the easy smile touch his lips.

"You're the reason I'm coming back here, but, Evie, I think you're mistaken about a few things. I'd give up everything for you, because if there was a choice between practicing law and you, you're my dream, you're my wife, so it isn't a choice. You're first and always will be—you and this baby." He rested his hand over her stomach, where the baby was growing.

The lump in her throat came out of nowhere, and her eyes burned from the tears that popped. She had never been an emotional wreck, and his thumb brushed at a tear that leaked out.

"So is this a tear of being happy we're going to move back, or…?"

She realized he was teasing her. As she sat up, his arms went around her, touching her shoulder, and she lifted her face to him, sniffing. "Yes, I want to move back here. Thank you," she said, and he slid his hands over her cheeks and lowered his head to press a kiss to her lips. When he pulled back, she wondered what she'd see, but it was still there, the love he had for her.

"I love you, Danny," she said, and this time he pulled her into his arms, sliding her onto his lap, holding her.

"I love you, Evie. I promise you it will be okay."

Chapter 8

"That was a fantastic dinner you made," Chris said as he closed the door to his bedroom, and it was never lost on JD how he filled a room. It didn't matter what he wore; he was so damn attractive, and the way he looked at her, like right now, had her pinned to the spot where she was sitting in bed, a book on her lap, reading. He stepped over slowly, and she realized there was something about him that was different, relaxed. It was freaking her out.

"Thank you," she said. It actually made her feel important, considering her job was now just being a cook for everyone in his family. "I enjoy cooking. Not a big deal, really."

He was standing beside the bed, looking down on her, and she wasn't sure what he was going to say, as his gaze didn't waver. Then he sat down on the bed and faced her. "Heard you called your parents," he said.

She closed up the book and rested it on the bedside table. "Yes, I thought I should let them know about the baby," she said—and that she wasn't going back, even though her father had surprised her by apologizing for how he'd treated Chris, saying he'd back off and give them space if she'd only consider coming home. It hadn't been something she expected, but she had no intention of asking Chris to move back to Martin.

He nodded, but she didn't know what he was thinking. "You know I would never keep you from seeing your parents," he said.

"I know that, but I also know it would never work there."

He leaned over her, resting his hand on the bed over her legs. He was close, and she could smell his scent, the outdoors. Her eyes went right to his full lips, which were so close. He leaned in and touched his to hers. It was so intimate and tender, and she reached up and rested her hand on his cheek, over the whiskers he still hadn't shaved off. She wondered how much longer he'd let it grow. At the same time, he didn't seem as freaked out anymore. What had changed?

"I love you," he said. "I want you to know how important you are to me."

She didn't know what to say. He'd never said that, and it hit her then that he meant it. He really meant it. She hadn't expected that, not yet, even though she knew she'd fallen in love with him. She just hadn't known where he stood.

He allowed his thumb to trace the soft skin of her jaw, and she felt for a minute as if she was treasured by him. "And I wanted to talk to you about some things."

"Oh, what things?"

There it was, that easy smile of his that she missed. He glanced away as he sat up, and his entire expression took on a seriousness she hadn't expected. "I know things have been kind of up in the air here, and I haven't really settled on anything, but I'm going to be doing more here on the ranch with my dad. I'll pick up work again too at the feed store in town. They offered me assistant manager before I left. For now, we'll stay here, but I wanted—no, needed to check in, because I never really asked you how you felt about staying here. I never gave you an option."

That wasn't what she'd expected. "Who are you, and what have you done with Chris?" she teased. "You realize this is the first time you've asked me that. You have this way of just doing, as if I don't have a say. And now…"

By his expression, for a minute, he seemed a little taken aback. She reached over and rested her hand on his arm.

"I'm quite fond of your parents," she said, "and I don't know. With everything that's happened, and now being pregnant, I'm actually glad to be here, to have the support. Your mom is looking forward to this baby, and I kind of want her to be around to help. But what about you? I know you may not have said anything about getting back on the road and moving on to other places, but it's there, and it bothers me to think that I could be holding you back. We would be." She rested her hand over her stomach.

The look Chris leveled at her was intense, and he rested his hand over hers. "I don't know about the future, JD, but I want it with you and our baby…" A soft smile touched his lips, and for a minute, it seemed as if the reality of the baby wasn't as terrifying. "I had my fun traveling, seeing the country, which is how I met you. Stuff happens, and life plans change. I'm okay with that. You're my responsibility, the baby too, and it's not something I take lightly, but at the same time, know that you and this baby could never hold me back, so get that out of your head."

Then he reached into his jeans pocket and pulled out a small box. Her heart kicked up as he looked at it, and she watched him, knowing what it was but at the same time not really sure.

He flicked his gaze back over to her. "I should have done this before, long before now." He flipped open the box, and there was a gold ring set with diamonds in the band. He lifted hers out and reached for her hand. "You're my wife, and you should have my ring so that everyone knows you're mine." He slid it on her finger, and she just stared at it and then over to the one still in the box.

She reached for it as he held out his hand. "And you're mine," she said and slid the ring on his finger.

He pulled her close, kissing her deeply before pulling away just a bit. He rested his forehead against hers. "I know this marriage started out unusual and was far from expected. Maybe you were shell shocked and wondered how long it would last, but I need you to know there isn't anyone else for me. I may not have said it, JD, or showed you, and maybe I didn't admit it to myself, but you're the only one for me. I really do love you and this baby. My mom and dad aren't the only ones happy. It may have taken me some time to get my head around it, but…I think it's pretty cool."

She lifted her arms over his shoulders and slid her legs around as he moved his hands on her waist. She went up on her knees, pressing against him. "Really?"

His hand ran over her butt and the thin spaghetti straps of her nightgown. "Mm-hmm, so I think it's time we turn in for the night, and you can show me what a loving wife you can be."

She pressed her hand to his chest as he pulled her closer and kissed her neck. "You're such a rascal."

He kissed between her breasts and held her close. "I am, at that. But only for you, JD."

Chapter 9

Diana stepped into Danny's old room, which had been turned into a nursery for the babies. Sweet Ally had been born just six weeks earlier to Evie and Danny via an unexpected C-section, but mom and baby were fine. Then there was Sophie, who was five days old, an easy delivery for JD and Chris, who'd hovered for the last few weeks. As young as they were, Chris and Danny were going to be amazing fathers—and to Diana's delight, she had finally gotten her girls: granddaughters.

"You're not going to wake them again?" Jed asked as he rested his hand around her.

She leaned into him. "No, as tempted as I am. They're so beautiful and cute, but I'll wait until they wake up."

Jed patted her side and steered her from the room. "Come on, you. I want to give them their gift now, before one or both of the babies wake up."

Danny, Mark, and Chris were in the family room, sitting on the sofa. Both new fathers had a beer, whereas Evie and JD had moved to the living room.

"Danny, Chris, come in here. Mark, you too," Jed called out.

Diana just stood with her husband, in the circle of his arms, watching Danny and Chris, who'd grown into fine-looking young men. There was so much about them that resembled their father, not just in looks but in the way each cared for his wife and had become a protective alpha when his baby was born.

"Okay, we're here," Danny said, and Chris gave his brother a teasing shove. Something about Danny, a light-heartedness, had returned since he and Evie had moved back and begun living in the loft again. He'd passed the bar and was practicing law with Diana, and he was brilliant and happy.

"Your mother and I have something we wanted to give you, and we thought now would be the time. Danny, with you working with your mom now, and Chris, with you taking a lot off my shoulders, working this ranch and handling all the groups booking in, we thought now would be a great time to give you each a piece of land."

Chris was never one to show what he was thinking, but even he seemed a little surprised.

"You're giving us a piece of land here?" Danny said, and at the way he said it, Diana had to hide a smile. She knew they wanted something of their own, but this was better than perfect.

"Yup," Jed said. "So this is a big property. I'm giving you each two acres so you can build your own place, for your family, when the time is right."

She watched her daughters-in-law, Evie and JD, and then her sons, Danny and Chris. Something about this moment, she was sure, would make it a memory she'd cherish forever. As they each hugged their wives, Diana could see the happiness, the joy, that was there.

"And, Mark, one day there will be something for you, too," Jed said. "But, Chris, Danny, both of you, and, JD and Evie, you too, I just wanted to say from your mother and I that we love you and those babies, and I'm pretty sure Diana isn't going to be too eager for her granddaughters to be far from her."

Everyone laughed.

"Oh, we know, Mom," Danny said from where he stood with Evie in his arms.

"Just like I told JD," Chris said, "you always wanted that girl, and now you've got her in two granddaughters!"

Turn the page for a sneak peek of
IT WAS ALWAYS YOU the next book in The FRIESSENS
Available in print, eBook and Audiobook

She never realized until she lost him that he is the only man she'd ever love.

Katie and Steven were the love of each others lives until a tragedy and the fallout of Steven's injuries drove the couple apart.

They share a son, but Katie and Steven have moved on with their lives, dating other people, and neither has seen the other in five long years. But when Steven comes knocking on Katie's parents door after learning she is back in town, Katie is forced to face her estranged husband, the love they had that broke her heart, and his intentions regarding their all but over marriage are soon made very clear.

But the only problem is that as easy as it is for them to walk away, seeing just what it means to move on and start a new life may not be as easy as they once thought.

It Was Always You

CHAPTER 1

What was it about time? Looking back, Katy couldn't understand wanting what she once had. Now there was a sense of peace, certainty, and needing to close the door and finish something that she knew all too well had at one time gutted her.

Katy took in her nails, the manicure and teal polish she'd splurged on, and stepped out of her black Jeep. It wasn't new but was as close as she could afford, a few years old, a decent amount of mileage, with a backseat for Fletcher. She shut the door, gripping the stiff straps of her mint green bag and taking in the mix of sun and cloud, hearing a tractor in the distance, the singing of birds, and the lack of white noise that was constant in the city. She felt the breeze brush against her bare legs.

"Hey, you!" Emily said. Her mom was in the dirt on her knees with a flat of marigolds, planting them in the bed at the front of the house. "I didn't expect you. You should have told me you were coming…"

Everything looked so different.

Her mom brushed her hands as she stood up, sounding

so happy. Then, for a second, her smile faded. "Did something happen?" Emily said. There it was, the worry that seemed to be a constant for her.

"No, everything is fine, Mom. Just got off my shift on time and thought I'd slip down and see Fletcher, see how he's doing."

It was time for him to come home. There it was in the way her mom glanced to the side, a hesitation as she walked toward her. She had to know something was up.

"Is Dad here?" Katy asked as her mom held out her arms and hugged her after only another second, pulling her close, maybe unsure of how she looked in the pale blue shirt and faded jean shorts she had on.

"He's here someplace. So how long are you off work?"

"Until Saturday, then I have to be back. Listen, I really want to talk to you and Dad about Fletcher and…"

"Hey, I thought I heard someone drive in," Brad said as he stepped out of the house. "Your mom didn't say you were coming back."

He hadn't changed except for the gray in his hair, now more pronounced. He strode down the stairs, which creaked under his weight. He was so large, broad chested, a rancher to the core, wearing blue jeans and a deep blue shirt with the sleeves rolled up. It seemed as if he hadn't shaved today. He was still a handsome man, and the sweat stains under his arms didn't diminish that in the least.

"New vehicle?" He was walking over to her, taking in her and then the Jeep.

"Yeah, I had driven the Beetle into the ground. It was time, got a good deal." She could afford the payments and still pay rent, she thought, and not have to worry one more time about the mounting repairs her car had needed.

"Katy was just saying she wants to talk about Fletcher," Emily said.

Her dad hesitated before pulling her close and hugging her, kissing the top of her head. Her wispy blond hair was now touching her shoulders, having grown since she'd hacked off everything with a pair of rusty kitchen shears how long ago? The horror in her mom's expression, and her dad's too, would forever be burned in her mind. No, that was another reason to never let herself go back to being that other person. That person had died.

"Well, let's go in. Fletcher's at school and will be back on the bus soon. I'm sure he'll be excited to see you," her dad said.

Why was it, as she took in a home that had been a refuge to her for so long, that she now felt as if she were a visitor and had to wait to be invited in? It wasn't reasonable, she told herself, feeling a hand on her back as she strode toward the stairs in sandals. Her toenails matched the polish on her fingers. She knew it was impossible for Fletcher, who was now seven years old, to appreciate the trouble she'd gone through for him.

"Relax," Emily said. "You seem rather tense. You okay?"

Her dad pulled open the door and stared down at her. For a minute, she wondered if he expected her to fall apart. At times she wished everyone would do her a grand favor and forget they'd seen her at her lowest and most vulnerable, being open, raw, and showing something she never wanted to see in herself.

"I'm fine. Stop worrying." She forced a smile as she took in the exchange between her mom and dad. There it was: concern, worry, and something she didn't want to examine too closely.

She slipped off her sandals and stood barefoot, resting her purse on the chair by the hall table, taking in the living room, which hadn't changed—the furniture set, the western theme, the artwork on the wall that had been there forever.

Her dad slipped his hands in his pockets as her mom stood right beside him, and she wondered again why she felt like such a stranger in a place where she should have felt peace and welcome instead.

"Well, I'm just going to say it, since this waiting and dragging it out is torture and since there's no easy way," Katy said. "It's time Fletcher comes home with me, lives with me."

She could feel her heartbeat kick up. Her palms were sweating. Her dad's arm was draped across her mom's shoulders, and the emotion seemed to make him dig in. She wondered why she'd thought it would be so easy.

"You want to take Fletcher back to Olympia now?" her mom said in a way that made Katy feel as if she'd suggested the most ridiculous thing. Before, she'd likely have backed down and shrugged and said never mind, but she couldn't do that. She'd struggled so long to find her voice again. It had been too long since she'd been back here, seeing her son only when her mom and dad had driven him up to see her, a day here and there, so few and far between. That wasn't how it was supposed to be.

"Look, I appreciate everything you and Dad have done for me, for Fletcher, but I'm his mother, and it's time he comes to live with me. I'm settled and stable now and have a good job. There's a school close by and a daycare at the hospital for when I'm working."

Her parents weren't smiling. She hadn't thought it would be this hard.

"Katy, let's just sit down and discuss this," her dad said and stepped forward, his arm out, his hand sliding over her shoulder and guiding her into the living room.

Just then, she heard a car outside, and she wasn't sure

what to make of the exchange between her parents, but it was something that had her stomach squeezing, bringing that familiar anxiety back. She had to remind herself she was a strong, confident woman, and she couldn't bury her head in the sand and ignore the things she didn't want to face anymore.

There were heavy footsteps as someone jogged up the steps, then a sharp rap on the screen door before it squeaked open.

"Hey, I know I'm early."

The deep voice had her freezing where she was, taking in a man she'd once been married to, had loved so deeply, and hadn't seen in years.

"I had no idea Katy would be here," he said, glancing to her dad and mom.

She wasn't sure what it was in the exchange, what it was in his expression for her, but it was something that now had her feeling as if she were the uninvited guest.

"No one knew," she said. "I had the time off work and decided to just drive down." She felt ridiculous for having to explain. She should ask him how he was, say something about how he looked. Good Lord, he looked fantastic. She hadn't expected him to look so healthy, fit, strong, and damn attractive. She heard the scrape of whiskers and knew it was her dad running his hand over his chin, but she couldn't take her eyes off Steven and how good he looked.

His dark hair was short and a little on the messy side, and he was tall, with broad shoulders. It seemed as if he'd filled out more, put on more muscle, and she realized he didn't have a cane anymore. In fact, the way he'd come in the house, strode in, it was as if he was the same old Steven, before the accident, before their lives had been ripped apart. No, scratch that—better than before.

"Well, then, I guess this would be a good time for a talk," Steven said. "Was planning on reaching out to you, Katy, because it's long past time we settled things between us." He glanced only once to Brad, and she saw how close they were. Why did that bother her so much?

"I wanted to talk to you as well, Steven," she said. Her heart was hammering, because he was a part of her past now. She'd put him on the back burner and had put this off for so long, afraid of ending that chapter of her life. Why? She couldn't say for sure, but at the same time, she knew with certainty it was time.

He was wearing faded jeans, and his T-shirt was one she didn't recognize. When he took a step to the side and lifted his hand, she took in the bare finger where his wedding ring used to be. Her ring. What was the matter with her?

"Great, then we should get started." Steven gestured toward the sitting area, and she heard her dad clear his throat.

"I'm not sure this is the right time, Steven," he said.

That had her attention as she glanced between them. The man she'd loved forever pulled his arms across his broad chest, tucking his hands under his armpits, and shrugged.

"I think this has been put off for too long," Steven said. "It's better it's out in the open, anyway, so we have some closure."

For a minute, she could feel the floor beneath her feet softening as she felt herself being ripped back to the young woman who'd hit rock bottom and clawed her way out of a place that was as low as anyone could go. "I agree, Steven," she said, "which is one of the reasons I'm here."

"Great, then we're on the same page. It's time we end

this marriage once and for all, sign the papers, and we can walk away and both get on with our lives."

She couldn't believe he'd said the one thing she'd been fighting for the courage to say, the one thing she'd rehearsed for how long? Her hands were hanging loosely, and she heard the squeak of the door and footsteps.

She turned to see Corinne Johnston, dark haired, slim, with dimples in her cheeks and that beauty queen package —her former best friend from school.

"Hi, Katy," Corinne said, appearing shy as she stepped over beside Steven, her hand slipping in his, the exchange between them close.

Like, WTF?

"Did you tell her?" Corinne asked.

Of course, instead of being relieved now, she was expecting the worst.

"Not yet…" Steven said.

Her dad stepped in closer as if he felt the need to get between them. "Steven." That was all Brad said, and it sounded much like a warning.

For a second, she wanted to run out the door and jump back in her Jeep and drive away so she didn't have to hear what he had to say, but she couldn't tear her eyes away from their linked hands and the flash of a diamond on Corinne's ring finger. *No, it couldn't be.*

"I can't put it off anymore," Steven said. "This has to happen now. I'm sorry, Katy. Corinne and I are getting married, so I want a divorce. We've been apart a long time, and this is merely a formality now. You have to know that."

Hadn't this been exactly what she'd wanted, what she'd wanted to say? She couldn't get her tongue to move, couldn't get her mind to form one reasonable thought. Everything she'd rehearsed and planned had completely left her head.

Then there were voices and chatter outside and little feet pounding on the stairs. "Daddy, Daddy!" she heard Fletcher shout as he raced in and over to Steven.

Steven beamed and hugged her son, and Corinne smiled down on him, touching his head as if he were hers. This was worse than anything.

"Hey, Fletcher," Katy said. Her throat was so dry, and she barely recognized her voice as she forced herself to speak, for a second worried that he wouldn't want her, but there was the smile he had just for her.

"Mommy!" he said as he raced over to her and hugged her.

She took in her mom and dad, and Steven and Corinne, and whatever it was in their faces staring back at her. This wasn't going to be as easy as she'd planned, and there was also the fact that she still needed to tell them about David and the promise she'd made—a promise she didn't know, right now, if she could keep.

About the Author

"Lorhainne Eckhart is one of my go to authors when I want a guaranteed good book. So many twists and turns, but also so much love and such a strong sense of family."

(Lora W., Reviewer)

New York Times & USA Today bestseller Lorhainne Eckhart is best known for writing Raw Relatable Real Romance where "Morals and family are running themes." As one fan calls her, she is the "Queen of the family saga." (aherman) writing "the ups and downs of what goes on within a family but also with some suspense, angst and of course a bit of romance thrown in for good measure." Follow Lorhainne on Bookbub to receive alerts on New Releases and Sales and join her mailing list at Lorhainne-Eckhart.com for her Monday Blog, all book news, giveaways and FREE reads. With over 120 books, audiobooks, and multiple series published and available at all, retailers now translated into six languages. She is a multiple recipient of the Readers' Favorite Award for Suspense and Romance, and lives in the Pacific Northwest on an island, is the mother of three, her oldest has autism and she is an advocate for never giving up on your dreams.

"Lorhainne Eckhart has this uncanny way of just hitting the spot every time with her books."

(Caroline L., Reviewer)

The O'Connells: *The O'Connells of Livingston, Montana are not your typical family. A riveting collection of stories surrounding the ups and downs of what goes on within a family but also with some suspense, angst and of course a bit of romance thrown in for good measure. "I thought I loved the Friessens, but I absolutely adore the O'Connell's. Each and every book has different genres of stories, but the one thing in common is how she is able to wrap it around the family, which is the heart of each story." (C. Logue)*

The Friessens: *An emotional big family romance series, the Friessen family siblings find their relationships tested, lay their hearts on the line, and discover lasting love! "Lorhainne Eckhart is one of my go to authors when I want a guaranteed good book. So many twists and turns, but also so much love and such a strong sense of family." (Lora W., Reviewer)*

The Parker Sisters: *The Parker Sisters are a close-knit family, and like any other family they have their ups and downs. Eckhart has crafted another intense family drama… "The character development is outstanding, and the emotional investment is high…" (Aherman, Reviewer)*

The McCabe Brothers: *Join the five McCabe siblings on their journeys to the dark and dangerous side of love! An intense, exhilarating collection of romantic thrillers you won't want to miss. — "Eckhart has a new series that is definitely worth the read. The queen of the family saga started this series with a spin-off of her wildly successful Friessen series." From a Readers' Favorite award—winning author and "queen of the family saga" (Aherman)*

Lorhainne loves to hear from her readers! You can connect with me at:
www.LorhainneEckhart.com
lorhainneeckhart.le@gmail.com

The Outsider Series
The Forgotten Child (Brad and Emily)
A Baby and a Wedding *(An Outsider Series Short)*
Fallen Hero (Andy, Jed, and Diana)
The Search *(An Outsider Series Short)*
The Awakening (Andy and Laura)
Secrets (Jed and Diana)
Runaway (Andy and Laura)
Overdue *(An Outsider Series Short)*
The Unexpected Storm (Neil and Candy)
The Wedding (Neil and Candy)

The Friessens: A New Beginning
The Deadline (Andy and Laura)
The Price to Love (Neil and Candy)
A Different Kind of Love (Brad and Emily)
A Vow of Love, A Friessen Family Christmas

The Friessens
The Reunion
The Bloodline (Andy & Laura)
The Promise (Diana & Jed)
The Business Plan (Neil & Candy)
The Decision (Brad & Emily)
First Love (Katy)
Family First
Leave the Light On
In the Moment
In the Family

In the Silence
In the Charm
Unexpected Consequences
It Was Always You
The First Time I Saw You
Welcome to My Arms
Welcome to Boston
I'll Always Love You
Ground Rules
A Reason to Breathe
You Are My Everything
Anything For You
The Homecoming
Stay Away From My Daughter
The Bad Boy
A Place of Our Own
The Visitor
All About Devon
Long Past Dawn
How to Heal a Heart
Keep Me In Your Heart

The O'Connells
The Neighbor
The Third Call
The Secret Husband
The Quiet Day
The Commitment
The Missing Father
The Hometown Hero
Justice
The Family Secret
The Fallen O'Connell
The Return of the O'Connells

And The She Was Gone
The Stalker
The O'Connell Family Christmas
The Girl Next Door
Broken Promises
The Gatekeeper

The McCabe Brothers

Don't Stop Me (Vic)
Don't Catch Me (Chase)
Don't Run From Me (Aaron)
Don't Hide From Me (Luc)
Don't Leave Me (Claudia)
Out of Time

A Billy Jo McCabe Mystery

Nothing As it Seems
Hiding in Plain Sight
The Cold Case
The Trap
Above the Law
The Stranger at the Door
The Children

The Wilde Brothers

The One (Joe and Margaret)
The Honeymoon, A Wilde Brothers Short
Friendly Fire (Logan and Julia)
Not Quite Married, A Wilde Brothers Short
A Matter of Trust (Ben and Carrie)
The Reckoning, A Wilde Brothers Christmas
Traded (Jake)
Unforgiven (Samuel)
The Holiday Bride

Married in Montana
His Promise
Love's Promise
A Promise of Forever

The Parker Sisters
Thrill of the Chase
The Dating Game
Play Hard to Get
What We Can't Have
Go Your Own Way
A June Wedding

Kate & Walker
One Night
Edge of Night
Last Night

Walk the Right Road Series
The Choice
Lost and Found
Merkaba
Bounty
Blown Away: The Final Chapter

The Saved Series
Saved
Vanished
Captured

Single Titles
He Came Back
Loving Christine

For my German Readers

Die Außenseiter-Reihe

Der Vergessene Junge

Der Gefallene Held

For my French Readers

L'ENFANT OUBLIÉ

9 781990 590108